THE LAST STAND

Bogan thrust out his gun and began firing down the ditch, where the Federals had raked them from a bridge, but the battle was unequal and the legion was giving ground when Bruce Whittle leaped up from his place.

Across the flat, between them and the guard-house, there stood a long, low adobe house, a fortress in itself, and, while the legion looked doubtfully after him, he made a run for it. The time had come for which he had longed, when he could put his courage to the test, and, as bullets zipped by him or tore up the ground, he charged straight into the storm of gunfire.

Other *Leisure* books by Dane Coolidge:

SNAKE DANCE
BITTER CREEK
THE WILD BUNCH
MAN FROM WYOMING

THE SOLDER'S WAY

WAY

Dane Coolidge

LEISURE BOOKS NEW YORK CITY

A LEISURE BOOK®

December 2007

Published by special arrangement with Golden West Literary Agency.

Dorchester Publishing Co., Inc.
200 Madison Avenue
New York, NY 10016

ISBN 10: 0-8439-5989-4
ISBN 13: 978-0-8439-5989-5

The name "Leisure Books" and the stylized "L" with design are trademarks of Dorchester Publishing Co., Inc.

Printed in the United States of America.

10 9 8 7 6 5 4 3 2 1

Visit us on the web at www.dorchesterpub.com.

The Soldier's Way

EDITOR'S NOTE

The text of this story, based on the Gringo Battalion in Pancho Villa's army, was taken from the second-draft typescript with holographic corrections and additions made by Dane Coolidge. An earlier version appeared as a four-part serial in *The Popular Magazine* (4/7/17–5/20/17). The author made no attempt to publish the story in book form, despite having prepared the typescript to do so, and thus this marks its first appearance. Acknowledgment is made to Mary A. Whittier, trustee of the Estate of Dane Coolidge, for having supplied the second-draft typescript of this story.

CHAPTER ONE

The tidings of war were in the air when into the plaza at Del Norte, where adventurers from all over the world had gathered, there drifted yet another derelict. He was young and straight and dressed in decent black, but the wild look was there in his eyes. Many glanced at him curiously as he sat by the old cannon, his emotional face drawn with pain, his tapering hands clutched before him, and one man turned and looked again at his hands. It was Sergeant Bogan, recruiting agent for Montaño and his Army of Liberation, but he passed on and bided his time. The hands were soft and slender, yet full of supple strength, the signs of a high-grade mechanic, but the man himself was too fine. There were other derelicts, already starved and broken, who would enlist for the price of a meal—the white-handed stranger could wait.

The sun had sunk low behind the Mexican Sierras, where the Army of Liberation lay hidden, when Bruce Whittle roused up from his thoughts. The light of his world had been put out suddenly and night was closing in upon him; there was a great pain in his breast and the memory of a kiss that was driving him to black despair. He rose up suddenly and that evening in Fronteras, across the river in Mexico, Beanie Bogan saw him playing the games and marked him for his own. The games were crooked, and, when a man lost, he was generally ready to enlist. Bogan drew in closer, glancing out from beneath bushy eyebrows like a watchful, rat-catching terrier, and at last the final card was turned. Whittle rose up slowly, his eyes on the cheating dealer, a fighting snarl on his lips, and then he clutched at the stakes.

"You can't rob me!" he cried.

As the dealer reached for his pistol, Whittle slapped him across the face. There was a loud report, a crashing of tables, and a rush of feet for the entrance, and then, as the house was plunged into darkness, strong arms seized Whittle from behind and dragged him out a side door.

"Nix! Nix on that stuff!" panted a hoarse voice in his ear. "The *rurales* will get you, sure. Stand up . . . you ain't hurt . . . and now beat it for the river or you'll rot in a Mexican jail."

Whittle's knees were trembling, his strength had fled, but at the word *jail* he shook himself free.

"No, no!" he gasped. "I'd die! I couldn't stand it!" And led by the resolute Bogan, he ran until they crossed to Del Norte.

"Now," said Bogan as he led him to a card room and poured out a glass of liquor, "drink that, and tell me what's the idee."

"I don't drink," answered Whittle, and, sinking down in a chair, he buried his face in his hands. Death had been so near, and yet it had passed, and now he was weak and faint.

"Oh, I see," observed Bogan, and pulled down his lip.

"You see what?" demanded Whittle.

Bogan evaded the question by raising his glass in the air. "Here's to 'em," he said enigmatically.

"To whom?"

"To the women, God bless them. If it wasn't for them, I'd lose many a likely recruit."

A flush of anger came over Whittle's pale face and mounted to the roots of his hair. "You take too much for granted," he answered shortly, but Bogan shook his head.

"Nope," he said, "when it isn't booze, it's always a woman that drives a man to . . . that." He jerked his head in the direction of Fronteras, and Whittle reached for his glass.

"You are mistaken," he said, and drank down the whiskey. "Now who are you and what do you want?"

"That's the stuff!" Bogan applauded. "Put it down and have another, and I'll let you in on something good. You're a mechanic, ain't you? I knew it by the look of you . . . and perhaps you're a pretty good shot? Well, how would you like now to join Montaño's army and come out and help fix our guns?"

"What? Enlist as a soldier? In the Mexican army?"

"Ah, nah, nah!" burst out Bogan impatiently. "You don't get the idee at all. I'm Montaño's agent and I'm raking the town for recruits for the Foreign Legion. He's got lots of Mexes but it's Americans he's after, and he pays 'em two hundred a month. Two hundred dollars gold, and everything found, and a cracking good horse to ride, and, when we take Fronteras, as we will in jig time, you'll come in for your share of the loot. And when the war is over, if you stand by the chief, you get a nice little Mexican girl and a grant of good land to boot. Nah, listen, now. Didn't I follow you over to that gambling house and keep you from getting killed? Well, then, where's your gratitude?"

He sat back and thrust out his jaw belligerently, but Whittle did not reply. He was living in a daze in which some things were clear and others far away and confused, but he felt no obligation of gratitude. Left alone, his troubles would have been over. Not only that but *she* would be free, with only his memory to haunt her. But now—he regarded his rescuer malevolently.

"Why should I thank you for that," he asked, "when I did it on purpose to get killed?"

"What? A fine-looking young feller like you? *Ahh*, forget it and take a drink! Nah, drink your whiskey and listen to me now . . . don't go and get killed for no woman! They ain't worth it . . . none of 'em. And here's another thing, pardner. Things always look different the next day. You may be cast down now but tomorrow you'll feel different . . . and there's nothing to kill grief like a good fight. When you're up in the saddle and the boys are all yelling and you ride down on 'em like a bat out of hell, what's a woman then, or anything else? And if you go out, you die like a man."

He nodded grimly, and, as Whittle's eyes gleamed, he laid back his old Army shirt.

"Look at that," he said, and showed three lines plowed like furrows through the shaggy hair of his breast. "Machine-gun fire," he boasted, "over at Villa Nueva, but do you think I laid down and quit? I did not," he affirmed, "and, when I cash in, I'll take a few Mexicans with me." He swelled out his chest and his little green eyes snapped and sparkled with a daredevil smile.

"Tell me about it," said Whittle hoarsely. "Did many of your men get killed? And how did you happen to escape?"

"Now you're talking like a man," observed Bogan cheerfully. "Take another drink and we'll make a soldier out of you yet. It was badly handled, because Montaño's no general, but here's the way of it . . . we was making a night attack. Buck O'Donnell was in the lead with his belt full of bombs, and all the fighting Irish at his back. Then come Montaño and the rest of the Mexicans and the street was as dark as a pocket. Up the *calle* we slipped, never making a sound, until we see the *cuartel* just ahead . . . and then *hurrr-rup*, she broke loose from up on the roof and they mowed us down like grass. We went down in a bunch, with me underneath, and three bullets just cut my breast. Sure we'd planned a surprise, but the Federals was waiting for us . . . some yaller-belly had tipped 'em off. I laid there a minute till they'd run through their first clips, and then I rose up and run. There was a barbed-wire entanglement between me and the brush, but I sifted through it, leaving most of my clothes, and never stopped till I got to the river."

"And the others?" asked Whittle.

"Some got to a house and made a stand, but it was battered down with artillery. There was seven got away, out of thirty-odd Americans, and Montaño himself got hit twice."

"Then why do you go on? Are you interested in the revolution or . . . ?"

"No, here's the point," expounded Bogan. "I'm a soldier, see? And a soldier does his duty. He never quits, and he never weakens, and he takes a proper pride. Three months ago I was over at the fort . . . top sergeant in B Company of the Seventh . . . when this ruction broke out down below. Montaño sent an agent to take on some experienced men and O'Donnell and the bunch of us bought out. We'd seen service before, in Cuba and the Philippines, and we were crazy to mix in on the game, but the Federals proved too much for us. We were badly led and they wiped us out, but they learned that the *gringos* can fight. We walked up to their guns, and even then we didn't quit, and we're going back again! What say, do you want to sign up?"

He whipped out a paper and laid it before Whittle while he ran on with his recruiting patter.

"You don't join no Mexicans. You join the Foreign Legion, made up exclusive of white men. Gambolier is in command and he's a titled Frenchman that has been through their military schools. Every man that joins is a soldier and a gentleman and I can promise you active service at once. I'm sending 'em across, ten or twelve every night, and the peons are flocking to our banners. All Mexico is in revolt, the Federals are deserting, and their commands are confined to the large towns. We've got three thousand men within twenty miles of Fronteras and this time we're going to take the town. If you take on now, you get two hundred a month and. . . ."

"All right!" cried Whittle, carried away by some madness. "I'll go . . . and I'll never turn back."

"That's the boy!" cheered Bogan, thrusting the pen into his hand. "Sign your name right there on that line. And now, come on, the boys are waiting to go across."

He rose up and started for the door, but Whittle drew back and hesitated.

"What? Are we going to start now?" he asked.

"That's right. I'll take you down to Rico's place . . . that's the dump where we keep the men . . . and we'll cross up the river, about midnight. That is, unless you want to stop over, and you won't, when you see the joint. It's full of dirty, stinking Mexicans and fighting shanty Irish, all hollering for booze at once. We have to take all kinds, you know. But come on. What are you stopping for now?"

"I want to write a letter," answered Whittle doggedly. "And . . . I'd like to be alone."

"Huh, some skirt," muttered Bogan as he fidgeted outside the door, "but I'll wait . . . he's worth ten dollars to me, when he's crossed."

He paced up and down, went out and got a drink, and came back and peered in through the door. His soldier of fortune had his head on the table and the paper lay before him, untouched.

CHAPTER TWO

The cold night wind was whipping down the street, whirling dust and flying papers before it, when Whittle stepped out of the saloon. They were in the low part of town where, along the edge of the river, the Mexicans had built their flat adobe huts as thickly as mud wasps' cells. At one side lay a canal, flowing deep with muddy water, and the railroad track running beside it. Beyond that, gleaming faintly in the light of the stars, rushed the current of the shallow Río Grande. Across it lay old Mexico, with its warfare and brigandage, its romance, its mystery and—death. Whittle gave himself up to melancholy forebodings and followed along after Bogan.

They hurried up the river, looking down from the railroad track at the sleeping mud houses on both sides, until at last, before a house more pretentious than the rest, Beanie halted and struck a match. He lit his cigarette, and then, as the flame leaped up, revealing his face for the moment, another match flashed from the doorway of the house, and a short man with a gun stepped out. He was followed by another, and, as he mounted the track, a line of furtive and huddled figures came stooping through the door. Two or three were Americans but the rest were Mexicans, muffled up to their eyes in their blankets, and, as Brogan spoke in Spanish to the short Mexican called Rico, he looked them over carefully before he led the way up the track. Rico followed with his gun, reeking potently of mescal, and the rest fell in behind him. A mysterious confederate waved his hand from a boxcar; another man, not so friendly, plunged hastily into the willows at a threatening move from Bogan. Then, from within the black shadow of a cottonwood tree, there came the ringing challenge: "Halt!"

They halted, and, as a soldier stepped out from his shelter, Whittle turned and started to run.

"Here! Stop!" commanded Bogan, jerking him roughly back again. "Don't you know that sentry will shoot?"

And then the challenge: "Who's there?"

Brogan answered evenly: "A friend."

He advanced, as ordered. There were low words of greeting, and the sentry struck his gun with his hand.

"Pass, friend," he said, and stepped back into the shadow while Beanie went on his way.

There was a surety about his dealings with the sentry that showed him to be thoroughly at home, and, as the river swung north, he turned into a trail that led like a tunnel through the willows.

They came out suddenly upon a well-tramped path that led along the bank of the canal, and, as they rounded a point far up the stream, they came upon another sentry. Once more the old fear moved Whittle to think of flight, but, after a few low words from Bogan, the sentry resumed his post.

They stood upon the abutment of a low concrete dam over which the river water slipped and gurgled in a long, unbroken line. It was the diversion dam for the two canals that irrigated the low land along the river, but it could serve other purposes as well.

"Here's where you cross," observed Bogan briefly, and disappeared into the brush. With their shoes in their hands the timorous recruits waded, shivering, across the stream, and at last in the shadow of ghostly cottonwoods they landed upon the soil of Mexico.

"Here's to liberty!" spoke up Rico, taking a drink for courage, and then, with his gun at the ready, he led the way into the hills. Up a long, sandy wash that wound in between clay banks they toiled on in single file. The banks turned into walls and into towering cliffs that shut out the dim light of the stars, and, as the cañon opened out again, they saw all about them the jagged peaks of the Sierras. A pale half moon that had risen at midnight filled the valley with a deceptive light, and at a fork in the trail the half-drunken guide studied long, and turned to the left. Again the trail forked, and once more he took the left until he was traveling more east than south. The path became overgrown with brush and full of rocks, and, as the Mexican recruits began to dispute the way, Whittle saw that their guide was lost.

Rico quarreled with his compatriots in guttural Spanish, making threatening motions with his gun, until at last in a fit of drunken rage he cocked it and thrust it in their faces.

"¡*Esto camino!*" he declared, pointing at the trail defiantly and led them on through the night. All trace of the dimming path was lost; they climbed over ridges, fought their way through thorny bushes, and suffered thrusts from poisonous Spanish bayonets until finally, as the sky began to pale, they sank down and waited for the day. The guide was lost, he admitted it now, and no one knew the south from the north. The mountains were behind them, there was a great plain in front, but where was the camp of Montaño? The sky became light and dark again, and then, as the sun rose up above the rim of the plain, they heard the distant roll of a drum.

"¡*El campo!*" cried Rico, springing triumphantly to his feet, but, as he started across the plain, they were startled by the thunder of a cannon.

"What's that?" demanded Whittle.

They stopped and listened as a bugle call came to their ears. It was "Reveille," sounded by a full band of trumpeters, and the cannon was the morning gun at Fronteras.

"¡*Santa Maria!*" exclaimed the guide, crossing himself in a panic. Followed by the rest of the fugitives, he started on a run for the river.

The trumpets blared on, and, as they hurried across the plain, they could see the white houses of the Mexican town, and across the river, rising high against the dawn, the American city of Del Norte. In his drunken wanderings Rico had struck a circle and nearly delivered them to their enemies. The Army of Liberation was far to the west, beyond the jagged Sierras, and they, without even the guns with which to fight, were still within sight of Fronteras.

The Mexicans led the way, running along the base of the hills toward the clean line of treetops to the north, but their haste was their own undoing. A cloud of dust rose up on the outskirts of Fronteras, rushing straight across the plain, and soon against the white of its mantle they could see the bobbing heads of horsemen. It was a troop of *rurales*, the rangers of Mexico, and they were riding to cut them off. Long and anxiously they had looked to the west for the vanguard of an army and this huddle of men, fleeing wildly for the border, could be nothing but a band of Montaño's followers.

They came on, yelling, and, at a warning volley of shots, Rico wheeled and discharged his gun defiantly. It was a single-barreled shotgun of the cheapest grade but at the loud report the *rurales* pulled up for a conference.

"¡*Adelante!*" cried the guide heroically, and, led now by the frightened Mexicans, he ran with all his strength toward the river. But the *rurales* had recovered from their surprise, and, seeing them again in full flight, they came on after them at a gallop.

"*Ay*, Santissima María," moaned Rico, and, at last overcome by exhaustion from his debauch, he staggered and dropped to the ground. "Oh, help me," he implored as the Americans toiled past him. "Do not leave me here to die! Oh, you, sir!" he cried, holding out his hands to Whittle, and at the fear in his eyes Whittle stopped. He was not afraid although he fled with the rest, and, catching up Rico's gun, he fired at the spurring horsemen. They were close upon him, strung out along the trail, and the buckshot raked their column like hail. Horses reared and pitched, riders dropped their arms, and in the tumult all order was lost.

"Now run," said Whittle, and, raising Rico to his feet, he crouched down behind a rock. It had come, at last, that moment of exaltation of which Beanie Bogan had spoken, and, with his face to his enemies and a great joy in his heart, he waited to meet his death. The *rurales* had dismounted behind a low ridge, and, as he stepped out into the open, their carbines all spoke at once. But the shots were wild, and, at a shout back to him from Rico, Whittle turned and ran up the trail. They had missed and it was still in his power to save his comrades from disaster. The trail, pinched in between the encroaching hills and the broad flood of the Mexican canal, turned up now and cut along the slope, and, once over the point, they would be safe. He could see them running, with Rico behind, and, as he scrambled up the hill, he could hear the bullets as they struck into the dirt about him.

He won over the point and, taking shelter behind a rock, looked down to where the rest fled toward the river. It was a long way yet, across an open flat, but if he could hold back the *rurales*, the fugitives might swim across to safety. As the *ru-*

rales, by ones and twos, came spurring up the slope, Whittle rose up to meet their charge with his heart filled with a new, stern joy. Here was the death he had dreamed of, giving his life for others, dying clean and fighting like a man. He stepped out into the open, silhouetted clearly against the sky, and aimed at the foremost rider.

"Come on!" he cried, and pulled the trigger but the startled *rurale* did not return his fire. At the first outflashing of that figure in black, with the nickel-plated shotgun in his hand, he had wheeled his horse and swung down the slope in a mad effort to avoid the blast, but it caught him in full flight, burning his horse across the rump and sending him plunging down the trail. As he passed down the line, a swift panic seized those behind, and, riding in a disorderly rabble, they whirled around the point of the hill. Whittle stood there alone, still outlined against the sky, but death had passed him by. A great yell of cheering came from across the river, and, as he turned to look behind him, he saw the steep hills black with men. Across the broad flat the fugitives were running fast, with Rico still far behind, but the *rurales* were nowhere in sight.

Whittle loaded his gun and, settling down behind a rock, laughed grimly to himself. It was the joy of victory, of conquest and exulting, of seeing his enemies in full flight—it was a fitting prelude to death. From his post on the point he could see his comrades swimming, and fat Rico running down toward the dam, and then in a high, insistent yell the Americans began to call.

"Run, run!" they shouted, but why should he

stir from his place? He had turned back the *rurales* and he would keep them back until Rico had crossed on the dam. He stood on the point and looked across at the Americans, and at the automobiles that came rushing up the road. Men were coming from everywhere to witness the fighting, but the crowds on the hills were frantic, still beckoning with their hats for him to run. But why? The answer was the *ping* of a bullet and the smoke rising up from his rock. The *rurales* had been riding to get above him and now they were shooting down from the heights.

"Run! Run!" shrieked the Americans, and, as he shot back a challenge with his futile shotgun, he suddenly felt the call. He wanted to escape because they wanted him to escape, those Americans on the other side.

"All right!" he answered, and dashed down the trail, the gun still clutched in his hand. The bullets striking about him threw up little puffs of dust, they leaped and ricocheted ahead, but he gained the edge of the stream untouched. It was broad here and deep, held back by the dam, and, as he saw the muddy swirls and measured the distance, he sat down to take off his shoes. But now a shriller yell rose up from the crowd, and, across the flats from where they had crept up through the brush, there came racing a band of *rurales*.

"Jump!" shrieked the crowd, and, as Whittle plunged in, he saw soldiers in khaki line the bank. They were the border patrol, placed along the river to prevent any violation of neutrality, and they stood with their guns raised to protect him.

He came on bravely, using a racing stroke and fighting to pass the middle of the stream, but when a bullet cut the water beside him, he dived and swam with the current. 100 feet below he thrust up his head, gasped in air, and was gone again, and, when he rose, there were soldiers above him and guns pointing threateningly across the stream.

"Don't you shoot!" he heard the soldiers shouting, and, as he drew himself up on the bank, he saw the *rurales* riding furiously away. Then as soldiers and civilians hauled him out of the stream and slapped him on the back for joy, Beanie Bogan came fighting his way through the crowd and caught him by the arm.

"Hell's fire," he snarled, "do you want to get pinched? Well, come on then, and get out of this mob."

CHAPTER THREE

Bogan was cursing viciously as he dragged Whittle through the crowd and thrust him into an automobile found by chance.

"Drive downtown," he said to the startled chauffeur, "drive anywhere, till you get rid of these crazy lunatics." He slammed shut the door and pushed Whittle back out of sight while he shot back insulting denials at the crowd.

"Nah, of course he ain't here!" he snapped. "No, I don't know 'im . . . he's back with that bunch!" And then to the driver he added: "Speed 'er up . . . I'll pay your fine."

The machine leaped forward, and, as they thundered down the boulevard and twisted in and out through side streets, Beanie turned to his dripping recruit.

"Did, you see that big fat feller in the O.D. suit?" he asked. "Well, he's a gumshoe man for the Department of Justice. Another minute and he'd've had you pinched for violating the neutrality laws. Holy cats, what a hooraw! The whole town turned out . . . a regular battle . . . and half of 'em thinking it was Montaño. About a thousand men, all piping us off . . . and me supposed to be a secret agent! Well, we'll get you a new suit and switch the deal. How'd you like to help me run a few guns?"

"What . . . smuggle them across?"

"Yes, and put up a fight for 'em, if we happen to got jumped by the *rurales*. I'll get you another shotgun, being as you take to 'em so natural, and I guess we can cut it between us."

He was smiling now in a curious, twisted grin, and it suddenly came over Whittle that Bogan was tendering an apology.

"Why . . . all right," he faltered, and fell into silence for Beanie Bogan had not always been so friendly. On the night before, after persuading him to enlist, he had sent him across the line like one of a herd of cattle.

"I got you wrong," confessed Beanie at last. "I didn't think you'd fight." Then he spoke to the chauffeur who whipped down a back alley and stopped at the rear of a store.

Half an hour later Whittle stepped out a new man, attired for the rough work of a gunrunner from his sombrero to his tan-colored boots. "Now," said Bogan, "that's a little more like it . . . you don't look so much like a preacher." He slipped in the back door of a nearby restaurant, and, while the Chinaman rushed in a meal, he talked out of the corner of his mouth.

"Here's the idee," he explained. "Montaño has got the men, but danged if he can get 'em the guns. They've got shotguns and bean shooters, and little Twenty-Twos and everything but standard Thirty-Thirtys. The guns is on this side, you understand, and it's our job to get 'em across. All right, now this is what I want you to do. These Secret Service sleuths and Department of Justice agents will be watching every ford tonight but a good swimmer like you can take a wire across and we'll pass the guns over on a pulley. We'll do that up the river, where the cañon boxes in, and, just to keep the gumshoe boys busy send some Mexicans down to get caught. Just some dollar-a-day men with a few burned-out old Springfields to make it look good on the reports, and meanwhile we'll put over about a thousand new rifles and rush 'em into the hills for Montaño."

"How about the *rurales?*" asked Whittle doubtfully.

Bogan waved them aside. "All scared of the dark. They never come out at night . . . and every country Mex is our friend. Do you get the idee? If you ever run across one, just tell him you're working for Montaño. We'll pull this off tonight so you better go down to Rico's and get all the sleep you can . . . and here's a little money to skate on."

He passed over a wad of bills, winked wisely at the Chinaman, and slipped out again by the back door. Whittle finished his breakfast and passed out after him, but he did not go to Rico's. With his hunger satisfied, it came back upon him suddenly—that aching, voiceless grief that had driven him, half-maddened, to Del Norte—and he wandered back to the plaza. He had tried the solace of danger and adventure but it could not make him forget. He had loved a woman and she had married another. That he might learn to forget, but she had kissed him at the wedding—the bride's farewell kiss—and then something had stopped in his brain. She had loved him all the while, that glorious woman—so brave, so beautiful, so good—and he had not known till too late. And she had not known! He could see her startled look and—yes, he could remember their kiss. One kiss, no more, a greeting and farewell, and then he had turned and fled.

Once more, while the curious turned and smiled, he sat mutely with agony in the park, and, when he looked up, he saw—her! She was glorious still, but her eyes were saddened, and he rose up in horror at the change.

"Bruce!" she had cried, low and tender as before, but it woke only agony in his soul. "Oh, wait!" she had pleaded as he turned to flee. "No, wait . . . I have followed you here. It is not an accident . . . I wanted to tell you something."

"Ah, no," he had answered, his eyes set with anguish, "nothing matters now. What could you tell me that would change it . . . now?"

She did not answer for there, close beside her, appeared the raging face of her husband. He had come up unobserved, and, as he took her arm, he darted a savage glance at Whittle.

"Come, Constance," he had said firmly, "I cannot allow this to go on. You must return with me to the hotel."

"No!" she had cried, but, as he gazed at her reproachfully, she had submitted and turned away. A moment later, when she had stopped and looked back, her lover of a day had fled.

When Whittle came to himself, he was on a strange street and a Mexican Indian was plucking at his sleeve. He was a dark, powerful man in a faded soldier's uniform and across one cheek, like a brand on a horse, was burned the numeral 3.

"¡*Ven!*" he said, and beckoned with his fingertips, but Whittle drew away. "No . . . come in," coaxed the Indian, resorting to broken English, "Me Numero Tres"—he pointed grimly to his cheek—"me friend Beanie Bogan. You come." He smiled reassuringly but the scar on his face gave him a singularly sinister appearance.

"No," answered Whittle, and pushed him away, whereupon Number Three laughed indulgently.

"¡*Mira!*" he began as Whittle regarded him fixedly. "Me no Mexican, *sabe?* Me Yaqui Indian *de* Sonora. Good friend Beanie Bogan. You come . . . Rico's house."

He waited a while, and then, very goodnaturedly, he took Whittle by the arm and led him like a child down the street. They passed through narrow alleys, lined with squat Mexican houses made of mud and stray boards and tin cans, until at last on the very brink of the canal they stooped and entered Rico's hotel. It was a broad, low room, saloon and restaurant in one, and, as Whittle stood dazed in the doorway, a dozen men turned to stare at him. Then from behind the bar fat Rico came running and clasped him in his arms.

"Ah, my frien'!" he exclaimed, patting him lov-

ingly upon the back and striving in vain to kiss
him. "My frien', you have save my life!"

He turned and made a speech in exalted Spanish to the none too friendly Mexicans, and then,
taking pity upon Whittle' exhausted condition, he
assisted him to bed.

All that day, while Mexicans and American adventurers roistered and rioted in the room below,
Whittle lay in his room as if dead, but, as evening
came on and the recruits disappeared, he was
awakened by Beanie Bogan.

"All right, Whit," he said, flashing a lamp in his
eyes, "come out of it . . . it's time to get busy."

"What do you mean?" Whittle blinked, his
brain in a whirl. "Oh, I can't smuggle guns over
tonight."

"Yes, you can," answered Beanie cheerfully,
"and you'd better cross, too, or you'll see the inside
of a jail. The Department of Justice is looking for
you, sure, and there's some mug out there watching the door."

"What? Waiting to arrest me? Well, I'll never
take to . . . I'd go crazy, shut up in prison."

"Nah, I'll get you out," responded Bogan confidently. "Leave it to me, and don't make no row.
The people in this town are all for Montaño . . .
and, listen, he's right out in the hills. We can see
his scouts, and, there's nothing to it, we got to
cross them guns over tonight."

Whittle rose up in bed, and, as he sat staring
blankly, Beanie pressed a bottle to his lips.

"Take a jolt," he said, "it'll make you brave, and
I need you bad tonight. I had men out looking for

you all over town. Numero Tres said he thought you were drunk."

"No, not drunk," muttered Whittle, rising sullenly from his bed, "but . . . well, come on, but I'll never go to jail."

"Suit yourself," answered Bogan, and lingered warily behind, for he had seen a man in the shadow.

The night was black with a dusty wind blowing, and, as Whittle stepped out the door, he was startled by the clutch of a hand. It caught his right wrist and twisted it behind him, and then a pistol was thrust against his side.

"Come on," said a voice, "and don't make any trouble. I've got some papers for you."

"What do you mean?" demanded Whittle, setting his feet for a struggle, but the man did not answer directly.

"You're wanted," he replied, giving him a quiet shove forward, and then a shadow slipped out the door. An unseen hand wrenched the pistol from the man's grasp, and, as he went to the ground, Beanie Bogan leaped back and snaked him bodily through the door.

"Now, Mister Man," he said, beckoning quickly to Whittle, "we'll have a look at them papers."

"Who are you, sir?" blustered the man, struggling angrily to his feet. "I'll throw you in the stink house for this!"

"Never mind who I am," answered Beanie grimly, "but show me the papers for my friend."

"Well . . . ," began the man, and Beanie cut him short with a blow and a savage kick.

"You danged tinhorn detec!" he burst out violently. "You can't run no blazer on me! You ain't got no papers or you'd pull 'em and serve 'em! Now come through . . . are you working for Reyes?"

The man, a great hulking brute of a fellow, seemed to shrink as he met Bogan's look, and his eyes became furtive and scared. "Oh, no, sir," he cried, "I'm a private detective! I've got nothing to do with the war. I don't want you to think, sir, just because I came down here. . . ."

"Come here!" commanded Bogan, his green eyes glinting, and with rude and unnecessary violence he jerked the star from the detective's vest and threw it on the floor. "Now," he said thrusting out his jaw and balancing his revolver to strike, "come through or I'll bust your head. Who're you working for, and what do you want of my friend?"

"Why . . . a Mister Pedley . . . he. . . ."

"Pedley!" cried Whittle in amazement, and Bogan drew him swiftly aside.

"Who's Pedley?" he hissed. "Has he got anything on you?"

"Why . . . no," stammered Whittle. "I. . . ."

"Then you git!" commanded Bogan, and, throwing open the door, he kicked the detective into the street.

CHAPTER FOUR

The night of the big gunrunning passed like a dream for Whittle. He was conscious of being taken far up the river in a closed automobile, of guards hurriedly stationed and a cord thrust into his hand, and then of a long swim in the river. He landed and made fast the heavy wire that followed, and then a bundle of guns, hung by a hook on a pulley, came slipping across the cable. Swart Mexicans with pack animals appeared from the darkness and received the guns as they came, and swift-moving automobiles came purring out from Del Norte with load after load of burlapped rifles. When the pulley stuck or the cable fouled, he swam out and set it right, but his heart was not in the game. One part of his mind seemed to attend to the work with a wholly admirable calm while the other thought of other things.

What did it mean, this blind and feverish flitting, this fantasy that people called life? And was

it worth the living? Was it not better, with all his
dreams lost, with his days but an agony of vain re-
grets, to end it all swiftly in some chance Mexican
battle and to pass on to whatever there was? Was
it not better for her, now that she was married to
Pedley, to pass decently out of his life? To remain
was but to flee from the sight of her unhappiness,
to writhe with unworthy jealousy. She was married to him now, and what hope could the future
hold out? Only the prospect of anguish and base
humiliation at the hands of her cad of a husband.

At the thought of the detective and his crude attempt to arrest him a flaming rage rose up in
Whittle's breast. After he had retreated instantly,
as a gentleman should, without subjecting his
loved one to remarks, then to find himself pursued to some Mexican hovel and maltreated by a
private detective. A cheap detective, a mere man-
handler of the unwary, kicked about like a bum
by Beanie Bogan—and hired by this man who
had won her. In another age, when women were
property, Whittle would have retaliated and taken
her for his own, but the chivalry of the times in
which he lived demanded that he make no
reprisals. If he killed the husband, he could not
take the wife; all the world would shrink from
him, and the woman would deny her own love.
No, it called for a sacrifice, such as men made of
old to placate some austere god, but he would do
it for her. It was best for Constance that he should
pass out of her life, and, God willing, he would
die like a man.

A rattle of scattered shots burst out down the
river and the work jumped forward in a flurry;

men came running up the road to see what they were doing, only to be pushed back by the close-mouthed guards, and through it all, like a devil of energy, Beanie Bogan came and went with the guns. He was cursing now in a low singsong of fury, his voice rising up in a howl at the least opposition to his will, but when, above the whine of the pulley and the rushing to and from of his men, he heard a measured *tramp* down the road, he dropped his work on the instant.

"Out of here!" he yelled, scattering his helpers in all directions. "Hit the wind or you'll all get pinched! Up the road with your autos . . . let the guns go to hell! I'm through . . . here comes the patrol!"

There was a thunder of motors as the machines darted off, and then, as a squad of soldiers came trotting up the road, Beanie Bogan made a jump for the hook of the pulley and went flying across the cable into Mexico.

"Now get these guns away," he ordered as he landed "before the damned *rurales* get wise. *¡Andale, hombres! ¡Al campo! ¡Pronto!*" And with Mexican packers and American soldiers of fortune heaving at bundles and hauling at lariats he was up and away in the same furious haste that had characterized his movements for days. Up from the river bottom they rushed, on over a pass, and then down the other side into the narrow cañon that Whittle had been through before, until at last, shortly after dawn, they passed the outposts of Montaño's army.

It was camped in a valley on both sides of a riverbed, where at intervals appeared shining strips of water—an army and yet not an army. No sentries challenged, no guards paced their posts; there was no order, no discipline, nothing but a horde of men. They were gathered about their fires with their blankets over their shoulders in groups of eight or ten, low-browed and black-bearded, the wild mountain outlaws of the Sierra Madres who had rallied to the standard of Montaño. Beneath their high hats, which surmounted them like toadstools, they glanced out with keen, suspicious eyes, and Beanie Bogan, glimpsing several that he knew, became suddenly distant and grim.

"Holy Mother," he muttered, "I can see a quick finish now. These *hombres* are hungry, they're down to straight beef, and I shipped out a hundred from Del Norte. And them American boys! Say they won't do a thing to me, after making 'em the big talk I did. Huh, huh, two hundred a month and the best of everything, and look what these fellows have got. They ain't even smoking, and, when a man's out of tobacco, he'll fight at the drop of a hat."

He heaved a heavy sigh, yet without losing any grimness, and followed on with the pack train toward a ranch house that appeared in the distance. It was a low adobe dwelling, surrounded by corrals in one of which the Foreign Legion was camped, and at the door a lone American was standing guard beneath the Mexican flag.

"Sergeant Bogan to see the general," said Beanie to the orderly, but at the sound of his voice, there was an outcry from within, and Montaño the Liberator rushed out. He was a short, pale

man with one arm in a sling and a worried, harassed look in his eyes but at the sight of the
burlapped bundles on the mules they lit up with
sudden joy.

"Ah, Bo-gan, you have brought yet more guns!"
he exclaimed, and seized him by the hand. "How
many in all?"

"Six hundred, sir," replied Bogan, bringing his
heels together, but Montaño was no stickler for
form.

"At last!" he cried, and with a gesture of thankfulness he embraced him with his unhurt arm.
"Sergeant Bo-gan," he went on feelingly, "you
cannot imagine my difficulties. The Foreign Legion, they clamor for everything, but my people
they clamor for guns, guns, guns! Not money, not
food, not shoes and blankets, but guns to fight for
our liberty. And what of the good people in the
city of Del Norte . . . are they still favorable to our
cause? You astound me, I am delighted, and yet it
is what one would expect from those who are fa-
vored with freedom. Won't you come inside . . .
and bring your friend . . . we can have a cup of
coffee together."

"No, thank you, General," answered Bogan
stiffly. "Shall I deliver these guns to Gambolier?"

"Oh, yes, to be sure. But come and see me later . . .
we will be marching on Fronteras very soon."

"Very well, sir," returned Bogan, still trying to
keep his distance, and, as he beckoned his packers
toward the camp of the Foreign Legion, he grumbled under his breath to Whittle: "Well, that's
him. He may be a patriot, but, by cripes, he'll
never make a soldier."

By a smoky fire the scant twenty Americans who made up Beanie's boasted Foreign Legion were arguing and bickering among themselves, while off to one side, as isolated as Napoléon, stood the military figure of their commander. He was a trim, slender man, this Colonel Gambolier, dressed immaculately in an olive-drab riding suit, and at sight of Bogan he returned his salute with the elaborate precision of a foreigner. But before Beanie could report, there was a tumult around the fire and half of the men started toward him. They were hatchet-faced cowboys and a sprinkling of ragged hobos, but the men who stood out in the motley crowd were dressed in United States uniform.

There were three of them—a giant Scandinavian, a big, aggressive Irish corporal, and a rat-faced street gamin of a private who advanced with a sneer to meet Bogan. "Hello there, you big bum!" he called out with false cordiality, but Bogan looked him coldly in the eye. Knowing that trouble was coming, it was not part of his policy to postpone it by honeyed words.

"Who told you to desert from the United States Army," he inquired as he walked on past, "and bring the old uniform into disgrace?"

"Ah, listen to 'im," chimed in the other two soldiers, and then the rat-faced private grabbed Bogan by the arm and jerked him to an abrupt about-face.

"Listen here, Beanie Bogan," he shouted threateningly, "you can't pull any of that stuff on me! We're as good as you are, or any other man . . . and you got us to come down here yourself!"

"I did naht," snarled back Bogan, striking him indignantly aside, "and you lay off of me, Jimmy Sullivan! This is a peach of a mob for a Foreign Legion, but if you've got any remnant of military dis-cip-line, you'll allow me to report to the C.O."

He passed on and reported, while the legion gathered together and held a hasty council of war, and then he turned back to the fire.

"Well," he said, gazing about him sardonically, "I hear you've pulled off a mutiny. Why, hello there, Helge ... how's the Terrible Swede?" He made a quirk pass at the fair-haired giant who was regarding him with an accusative eye and poured out a cup of coffee from the pot. "Help yourself, Whit," he added, handing Whittle a cup, and sat down on a box to drink.

"I ain't no Swede," answered Helge deliberately, walking around to look him in the eye, "and you know I ain't, Beanie Bogan. I'm a Dane, and, if I'm a deserter, it vas you dat got me drunk."

"Uhn-huh," grunted Beanie. "Well, have your own way about it, but cut off them U.S. buttons."

"Vat, and vare my coat open?" demanded Helge fiercely. "Vell, you sure must think I'm crazy."

"Here, lemme talk to him," broke in the big Irish corporal, thrusting Helge out of the way. "I bet you I can get through to him. Now, you damned liar, where's that two hundred dollars we was going to draw down every month? We ain't got the price of a drink amongst us."

"Oh, you ain't, hey?" returned Bogan, putting down his cup and rising with business-like calm. "Then that proves you ain't drunk and you'll take back that word or I'll ram it down your throat."

He laid off his hat and advanced with stealthy swiftness, his left hand raised, his right by his hip, and the fighting fire in his eyes.

"Well, what's got you so ringy?" grumbled the corporal complainingly, backing off and looking around for support, but no man stepped beside him.

Bogan snorted contemptuously: "That's all right, Bill McCafferty. I been top cutter in B Company too long to let a corporal call me a liar. And more'n that, I ain't scared of the whole damned gang of ye." He drank off his coffee and, picking up a mess tin, dipped out some beans from a simmering pot. "You're a prize bunch of soldiers," he went on insultingly, running his eyes over the nondescript group. "How do you figure you're worth two hundred a month? Here I been up on the line, working day and night to cross over enough rifles to get you armed, and now, by grab, I find you sitting around the fire like a gang of slouchy hoboes in the jungle. You won't drill, hey? Well, how d'ye expect to fight when we go up to take Fronteras? Are you going to drag along like them poor, ignorant Mexicans with nothing above your ears but your hat? Ain't Montaño got nothing to do but go get your money and come and put it in your hand? By Jehu, if I was in his place, I'd can the whole biling lot of you, and go out and hunt up some *men!*" He turned toward Whittle, who was sitting at one side, and indicated him by a wave of the hand. "D'ye see that man?" he asked dramatically. "Well, he don't claim to be no soldier, but I seen him myself, with a single-barreled shotgun, stand off a whole troop of *rurales*. I can take him now, and that Yaqui Indian over there, and whip more Mexicans than all of ye!"

He grunted scornfully and went on with his eating while the recruits regarded him resentfully. "Huh, huh!" he burst out again, ignoring their mutterings. "I wish Buck O'Donnell was here now. Buck was a fighting man, and no mistake, but you fellers? You're a bunch of kids."

"Well," burst out Sullivan, "we might show some form, at that, if we only had some leadership. But here we sit, getting dirtier and lousier every day, while Gambolier and General Montaño dope out this high military strategy. If we're going to take Fronteras, let's go up and take it . . . but Gambolier won't make a move unless it's according to the theory."

"That is not quite fair," interposed Gambolier hastily, striding over from where he had been listening. "Sergeant Bogan, you know well, for you have seen actual warfare, that it is useless to expect any decisive results until we can maintain the offensive. But, in order to be effective, the attacking body must always be of superior force. Now, in an attack upon Fronteras, we might have advantage at first, but in the city of Chulita, not two hundred miles to the south, is a garrison of several thousand men, and, unless something is done to destroy the railroad and effectually prevent their approach, reinforcements will be rushed up, we will be attacked from the rear, and our forces will be compelled to retreat. So my recommendation to General Montaño, in my capacity as military adviser, is that we first send a force to destroy the railroad and then, having effectively isolated the city, return to attack Fronteras."

"Well, why don't you go ahead then and destroy the railroad?" rallied Sullivan "You march up to Fronteras, and then back to Chulita, and then you march somewheres else. We enlisted for fighting, but if it's just marching you want, any ordinary Mexican will do."

"You shall see fighting," returned Gambolier gravely, "but first we must perfect our plans. The battle of Villa Nueva was lost most disastrously through a lack of co-ordinated effort. The enemy by a forced march attacked from the rear . . . our brave general was surprised from the *cuartel* . . . and between those two attacks the valiant Foreign Legion was destroyed in a single night. We must plan better now, every movement must be perfected, and, when once more we go into battle, I trust we shall come off victorious."

"Why don't you *burn* them bridges?" challenged Beanie Bogan suddenly. "It don't take a whole army to scrap a railroad. Didn't Buck O'-Donnell, with two men to help, burn twenty-seven bridges in one night? Well, gimme five thousand dollars and a pardner to go with me and I'll burn them bridges myself."

"Ah, but Sergeant Bogan," replied Gambolier patiently, "you are not fully informed of the facts. It is true, indeed, that brave Buck O'Donnell did destroy, by surprise, many trestles, but that, you must remember, was on the branch line that connects Fronteras with Villa Nueva . . . and it could not be accomplished again. The line to Chulita is now heavily guarded, with military trains all made up, and, at the first sign of burnings, the alarm would be sent out and cavalry rushed to the scene. Moreover, the important bridges on the Chulita line are built on concrete piers that can only be destroyed by dynamite. And, the country being flat and the high bridges few, each bridge will be carefully guarded. I thank you, but it could not be done."

"Ah, you don't know Bogan," sneered Sullivan venomously. "*He* don't care how many they are."

"No," retorted Beanie, "I was just waiting for you, Sully, to say you'd go along with me."

"Oh, but look who you are," parried Sullivan dexterously, "a regular fighting fool, while I'm nothing but a lousy deserter. I don't claim to be no dynamite devil."

"You don't need to," returned Bogan. "We can tell by looking at you that you haven't got the nerve of a rabbit. I'll tell you what I'll do, Sully . . . you come along with me and I'll give you the whole five thousand. Or any one of you! Now, come on, you fellers that are so crazy for a fight . . . we'll split the jackpot amongst us. We'll shoot our way in and shoot our way out again, and the last man that's left takes the pot. Buck O'Donnell got ten thousand for burning the Northwestern . . . who'll take a chance on the Central?"

There was a pause, in which the Foreign Legion looked sheepish, and then a voice spoke up from behind.

"I'll go," it said, and, as Bogan whirled about, he met the somber eyes of Whittle.

"Say, get onto yourself," whispered Bogan hoarsely as he drew Whittle off to one side. "Are you off your nut, or what?"

"No, I'm not," answered Whittle, "but you don't have to go. I'd rather go alone."

"Go where?" raged Beanie as the Foreign Legion smirked. "Say, what do you know about bridge burning?"

"Nothing, much, but it will give me quick action and . . . I'll be glad to have it over."

"You're crazy as a bedbug," declared Bogan shortly, and pushed him out of the way, but at the end of an hour he came back.

"Say," he said, "you talk too much . . . you've got me in a hell of a fix. Montaño heard the news that I'd made my brag, and that you'd sort of took me up, and now it's up to us, cold. I won't make a move till there's ten thousand dollars put up in a Del Norte bank, but he's offered that much for the job. It's taking a chance, but for five thousand cash . . . well, I'm game, if you want to go along."

"Very well," said Whittle, and, his mind suddenly at rest, he lay down and slept like the dead.

CHAPTER FIVE

If Beanie Bogan was a victim of circumstances in agreeing to dynamite bridges, he concealed his chagrin behind a purposeful frown and overlooked none of the profits. In fact, from his cold-blooded insistence upon the money being put in escrow, it became evident to Gambolier and Montaño that he intended to come back to collect. Yet, even so, brave Buck O'Donnell had gone to his death with a money belt of gold twenties around his waist and his pockets full of bombs. Montaño had been present on that fateful night and knew what a hazard it was, so he gave Beanie a note to his fiscal agent and sent him on his way to Del Norte.

For three endless days Whittle watched for his return, the dull fever still burning in his brain, while about him the disgruntled soldiers of fortune kept up their wrangling debates. All up and down the valley, in scattered bands and companies, the Mexican patriots sat inert. At intervals they rose up at the yell of—"¡*Carne!*"—and rushed to claim their rations of freshly killed beef, or rode to and fro on their stunted ponies, roping cattle, catching horses, and raiding ranches, but of military discipline there was none. They were simply a horde of outlaws and adventurers, with nothing to hold them together but Montaño.

Every day the patriot leader went down among his men with his wounded arm in its sling, making promises, healing difficulties, and welding them together by appealing to their hatred of the dictator. He distributed the new guns, with strict admonitions not to fire a single useless shot; he discussed with the leaders the proper disposition of their troops when they should join in the assault upon Fronteras, but all the time he was waiting upon Bogan, for their blows must be struck together. On a certain date the bridges would be destroyed, the troops in Chulita would be cut off from the border, and then Fronteras could be stormed. So it had been planned by Colonel Gambolier, who had studied military strategy at St. Cyr. Fronteras must be isolated and then attacked in force, and then, presto, Montaño would have him a capital. Yes, more than a capital, a port of entry through which to import ammunition and arms. And then the United States, of course, would recognize him as a belligerent.

Such was the dream of the visionary Montaño but the whole fair structure, for the time at least, was based upon the promise of one man—the red-headed Beanie Bogan, that devil of fighting energy, who had promised to destroy the railroad, burn the trestles, and dynamite the high bridges, cutting off all trains for two weeks. If for fourteen days no troops came by train, that was to be proof that Beanie Bogan had performed his contract and he was to receive his $10,000. That was the American of it, of course, that harsh insistence upon payment, that cold materialism in the face of death. But the service was worth the price.

Bogan came on the third evening, leading a pack animal behind him loaded down with mysterious stores, and, while he conferred with Montaño and Gambolier, Whittle guarded the shrouded packs. There was dynamite in those kyacks, enough to tear down mountains and snuff out the lives of many men, and nitroglycerine, packed in cans and bedded in sawdust, and, besides the pick of the *insurrecto* horses, two rifles and automatic pistols. Powerful field glasses were slung on Bogan's saddle and he had provisions and huge canteens; everything was provided for that forethought could devise, yet to Whittle the journey meant only death. Bogan planned to escape, and Whittle hoped that he might, but for himself oblivion was enough. Life held nothing for him now but a great world-weariness, a surging and hopeless despair, and he welcomed the thought of the end.

To avoid curious eyes, they set out at night and rode southeast by the stars, Bogan leading the way with the pack horse behind him and Whittle bringing up the rear. They rode on slowly, stopping often to rest while Beanie studied out the landmarks ahead. At dawn, they watered their horses at a hidden spring and turned up a rocky cañon. The trail was not unknown to Beanie Bogan, for he had been campaigning with Montaño for months, and shortly after daylight he reached a high, sheltered nook where the grass grew rankly between the rocks. All day they lay, sleeping and waking, Whittle guarding the horses while Beanie watched the railroad through his glasses, and, at night, they rode on toward the south.

From bare rocky mountains they descended to a plain, swept clean by a cold, ceaseless wind, and, as day dawned again, they were hiding in the sandhills almost within sound of the trains. Whittle was worn with hard riding and the buffeting of the winds, but for hours Bogan lay behind a bush and studied the bridges through his field glasses. His eyes were bloodshot from night watching and lack of sleep but back in their depths the imps of destructiveness were dancing with joy at his luck. The track was lifeless, few trains came and went, and about the bridges the dawdling guards made no pretense of patrolling their posts.

Yet, for all that, the restless Bogan was not satisfied, and, as night came on, he saddled again and pushed on farther to the south. Fronteras and the border, with its protecting Sierras, were far behind them now, and they rode across bare, level plains. The water lay in pools and broad, shallow lakes, surrounded by snowy crystals of alkali and the bone-dry carcasses of cows, but, as morning approached, they came once more to sandhills and found shelter by a tank in a draw. The day was cold and raw, with a bitter wind that lashed up the dirt in clouds, but, as evening came on, Bogan returned from his watching with his burned lips drawn back in a grin.

"Fine and dandy," he observed, opening up the pack and bringing out a gunny sack of Giant Powder, "the fireworks begin tonight. There's a big concrete bridge across the arroyo up above here that it will take 'em a month to rebuild . . . and that ain't all I've got framed up for 'em, either." He laid out the sticks of sixty-percent dynamite and carefully bored holes in their ends, then he bit down a cap on the end of a length of fuse and thrust it firmly into a stick. "About four of these," he said, "if I can drill a hole . . . or more if they ain't confined . . . and the whole pier is gone up . . . *flooey*. But if they jump us too quick, it's up to you to make a fight while I plant a little can of this." He held up a can of nitroglycerine and his eyes glittered with a wild, fighting light. "Now, here's the dope," he went on confidently, "here's the way I figure to win. Montaño has agreed to surround Fronteras tonight and that will protect us from cavalry from the north. We'll blow up this bridge and that'll stop the troop trains, if they send any up from the south. That leaves us safe and we can ride back along the track, and see how many trestles we can burn. But if you've got any word to send to that girl . . . well, of course, accidents will happen."

"What girl?" demanded Whittle as Beanie looked at him fixedly.

Bogan indulged in a smile. "Oh, I'm hep," he said, "and I don't blame you a bit . . . I saw her when I went to Del Norte. She asked all about you, but, before I could put her wise, a big fat slob that acted like her husband came up and shooed me off. Of course," he went on as Whittle said nothing, "it don't make no difference to me, but, if you want to write some letter, I'll take it with me, and then, if anything happens to you, I'll give it to her."

"No, never mind," answered Whittle.

Bogan began to sing at his work.

If you'll listen, I'll sing you a sweet little song.
Of a flower that's now drooped and dead,
Yet dearer to me, yes, than all its mates,
Though each holds aloft its proud head.

He glanced up slyly and crooned on again, his voice more provocative than ever.

'Twas given to me by a girl that I know.
Since we met, faith I've known no repose.
She's dearer to me than the world's brightest star,
And I call her my Wild Irish Rose.

He paused to tie together four sticks of dynamite and wrap them up neatly with the fuse, and then, like an Indian who chants his death song, he burst into the high refrain.

My Wild Irish Rose,
The sweetest flower that grows.
You may search everywhere
But none can compare
With my Wild Irish Rose.
My Wild Irish Rose.
The dearest flower that grows.
And someday for my sake,
She may let me take
The bloom from my Wild Irish Rose.

He laid out a hammer and three short drills and bound them up tightly with a sack, and then went back to his song. Whittle stirred uneasily, then moved away, and at last he broke his silence.

"Say, sing something else," he suggested impatiently, and Bogan's eyes lit up with deviltry.

"All right," he said, and pulled down his lip as he essayed a song of the bogs.

Oh, pigeon-toed Nora O' Grady,
I kissed her and called her me darlint.
Oh, crooked-legged, pigeon-toed Nora O' Grady,
I kissed her and called her me darlint.
Oh, knock-kneed, crooked-legged . . .

Oh, shut up!" burst out Whittle in a rage.

Bogan looked up with a grin. "Sure, you're hard to suit," he observed. "But the divvle gets into me just before a fight, and I can think of nothing but the girls. It's me wild Irish blood . . . I'm hell for the women, and they's no denying the fact. Many's the fine girl I've known in the old country and here, and they's few of 'em that told me no. I'm a fighting fool, fearing neither man, God, nor devil, and in love I've a way of my own. You're a fine-looking boy, with all that black hair and the soft sad look in your eye, but I can tell you something about women. No matter who they are . . . if it's a fine lady, like her, or one of the other kind . . . they love a bold, masterful man. Take shame to you now, for wanting to die, and listen to a word of advice."

"I don't want any advice," answered Whittle sullenly, "and we'll talk about anything but her. You don't understand, that's all."

"Oh, I don't, eh?" jeered Bogan, rising up to look about, and then ducking down out of the wind. "Well, it's plain as the nose on your face. The lady, God bless her, thinks more of your little finger than she does for the whole carcass of her man, and, if you would meet her halfway, as she undoubtedly wishes, you could have her for saying the word. And as for *him*, the big slob, just give me the tip and I'll lay 'im on a slab in jig time. If it wasn't that I was caught on the streets of Del Norte with my hands full of dynamite and worse, I'd have pasted him in the jaw with all the pleasure of life, the dirty, insulting hound. You're my pardner now, Whittle . . . ever since I lost Buck O'Donnell, I've been looking around for a pal . . . and I tell you what I'll do. You forget this idee that you want to get killed and play the game out to win, and, if we get back alive, I'll attend to that husband, and you'll be happy as a lark, eh, boy?"

He slapped Whittle on the leg and laughed encouragingly, but Whittle drew away in horror.

"No, you don't understand," he repeated dully. "There's nothing for me to do but die."

"Well, then, tell me about it," urged Bogan. "Sure, what's the difference when you'll be dead in a few hours or less? If you don't ride like hell, they'll pick you up by dawn . . . and there's no mercy for prisoners like us. We're bridge burners, see? We're the kind of boys that they stand up against a mud wall, so tell me, and get it off your chest."

"No, just leave me alone," implored Whittle wearily, "I've thought it all out, and I know best."

"You may, and you may not," answered Beanie

somberly, "but she's sure a fine-looking woman. A man might fall in love with a woman like that, but it never happened to me. There was one girl, though, little Molly McQuade, that I've remembered for many a year. She gave me one kiss and the next I heard of her she was Sister Theresa in a convent. She loved me different from all the others, but I was wild and full of devilment and she never would kiss me again. Then I went to Cuba, in the Spanish-American, and, when I come back, she was gone. This lady of yours, if you don't mind me saying it, has the same devout look in her eyes."

"Ah, yes, she has," broke out Whittle fervently, his eyes staring fixedly at space, "and that's what you can't understand. She's different from other women. She's like a nun, she holds her vow above everything, and that's why she married . . . him. And if he should die through me . . . if you should kill him . . . I'd never see her again. She has high ideals. Her world is different. Killing him will make it worse."

"Yes, but what about accidents?" persisted Bogan. "That Pedley was trying to get *you*. Didn't he send that fellow down to Rico's to catch you, and probably drop you into the river? But you say nothing should happen to *him* now?"

"No. That would be worse than ever, because then I would have lost her . . . regard."

"Regard, nothing!" burst out Bogan. "She's wild for love of you, and there's something she wants you to know, but you, like a fool, are trying to kill it without even awaiting her pleasure."

"No, I came too late," he answered desperately,

"I have no rights in the case. She was pledged to him before I first met her . . . and that was only by accident. I was only a jeweler, and, when she entered our workshop, she didn't even notice who I was. I was just a workman in the little back shop where her wedding silver was being engraved, but, oh, I remembered her! I could think of nothing else, and at night, after work, I waited outside her house. But I came too late, and my case was hopeless . . . such women must marry within their class."

He paused and Bogan remained craftily silent for fear he wouldn't go on with the rest.

"Yes, I watched," Whittle went on at last, "and one evening I saw her come out. She carried a bag and slipped out secretly, but I followed her down to the station. When she boarded the train, I stepped on, too, and, when she got off, I followed. It was down at the seashore, where they had their summer home, and the next morning she came down to the beach to bathe. I was there but she did not observe me, and from the troubled look in her eyes it came over me that she was unhappy. She swam straight out through the breakers, as if she were never coming back, and my heart leaped into my throat. I rushed up to the bathhouse and hired a bathing suit and started out through the surf, but by that time she had started to come back. Then I felt all at once that I had no right to follow her and I kept away, out of her sight. I was nothing to her. She did not even know me, yet something still impelled me to watch over her . . . and the next day she went out even farther."

Bogan waited, unblinking, as Whittle fell into a

reverie, and at last he went on with his story. "Then came a day when the currents were treacherous and the bathers all kept close to the rope, but she swam out beyond the float. I swam out behind her and watched from the raft, and then, very suddenly, a powerful current set in and all the bathers were caught. They screamed and struggled, for it swept them up the coast like a river, but I could think of nothing but her. So I left them for the life guards and fought my way out to sea where I could see the blue of her cap. It was a long way to go, but I reached her and at last I gave her my hand. We were far out to sea, but I was still fresh and strong, and she had not yielded to fright. She was tired, that was all, from being out so long and from struggling against the tide, and I supported her with one hand, like a child. So I kept her afloat until she gained back her strength, and at last we swam back to a rock. She did not know who I was . . . she had not seen me watching her . . . and yet somehow she seemed to know me. And when we had landed and huddled down in a cave to escape the wind and cold, we talked like the greatest of friends. She did not thank me for what I had done, but we spoke of what life means, and death, and, as we sat there together, clinging closely for warmth, I felt that in some way she was mine. I felt somehow that I had always known her, and always loved her, too, but I dared not tell her so. In my bathing suit I was just a man, and she was just a woman, and we forgot all about the world. Then suddenly a boat appeared and there was no time, of course, to say what I had longed to say. She gave me her hand, and asked me to call on her, but the doctors hurried her away and I never saw her again . . . except once."

"Why not?" demanded Beanie after a brief, startled silence. "Didn't she tell you where to go?"

"I knew where she lived, but, when I called, her mother sent me away. I called three times, and then her father . . . they thought I wanted her money."

"Oh, cripes!" burst out Beanie in an anguish of exasperation. "Did you let 'em get rid of you like that? Say, boy, you'll never get by. And you let that big slob step in and cop her. My God, you deserve to die."

"Yes, I deserve to die," repeated Whittle bitterly, and buried his face in his hands.

"*Ahr*, crying!" taunted Bogan. "When did that ever buy you anything? Here, wake up. Do you know what you are? You're a plain damned fool. But listen to me, pardner, the cards ain't all out of the box. She's come down here to find you . . . what d'you want, more than that? Ain't she trying to make it all up? Well, then, buckle on these guns and bring along that dynamite and we'll shoot our way back to the line. And then. . . ." He paused and a long, ugly line began to form at the corners of his mouth. "Well, never mind," he said, "but I'd hate to be Mister Pedley."

CHAPTER SIX

As the sun went down, a red ball in the dust storm, Beanie Bogan became restless and distraught. He brought up the horses and fed them some grain that he had treasured in his pack for this night; he sorted his dynamite and wrapped it up carefully where it would be protected from any chance shock. As the darkness came on, he tied it behind his saddle and gave the rest of the burden to Whittle. Then he paced up and down before the guttering fire, twitching his lips and cursing to himself. It was the panic that comes to the bravest of soldiers when they wait for the hour of battle, and Whittle respected his mood. He, too, felt sick and faint of heart at thought of the work before them, but he was reconciled to his fate. His calm was that of a condemned prisoner who has confessed and been shrieved of his sins, and he steeled his nerves for the ordeal. When the moment came, whether in the thick of battle or at the end of a long pursuit, he prepared his soul to meet death bravely as a lover and a gentleman should. His fear was only of his own weakness of purpose, or that he would fail his partner in the pinch, for Beanie had tried to be his friend. What he suggested was impossible, his solution was crude, but even his offer to put Pedley on a slab must be regarded from his point of view.

The wind, which at sundown had lulled to a brief calm, sprang up suddenly with redoubled force, and, as the first howling blast swooped over their shelter, Beanie Bogan slapped his leg and leaped up.

"Good!" he said, and, making everything fast, he led the way down the gulch. For such work as his a raging blizzard was the best weather that could be desired and at every buffet and slash of the sandstorm he chuckled and muttered to himself. They turned up a cañon, full of wreckage and old timbers where some former bridge had been washed out, and at an angle in its course he reined in suddenly and pointed up the gorge. There it stood, dimly outlined against the sky, the towering steel bridge they were to dynamite. Two spidery arches rose up from the streambed, now dry and waterless from the drought, and gray and shadowy in the gloom of the cañon bulked the concrete piers that supported them.

"You hold the horses," directed Bogan, and, with his pistol at the ready, he glided off up the ravine. He came back running, shaking a hand as if it hurt, and swung up onto his horse.

"I slugged the sentry," he muttered to Whittle, and rode on up to the bridge.

In the storm and darkness it loomed black above them, and, as he led their mounts into its shadow, Whittle stumbled upon the body of a man. He was only a swarthy peon soldier, sprawled grotesquely where Beanie's fist had struck him senseless, and Bogan snaked him impatiently aside. Then, while Whittle held the horses and kept watch against surprise, he went swiftly about his task. By the side of the pier he laid out his drills, and soon, above the rush of the wind, there rose the measured strokes of his hammer. His back rose and fell in a ceaseless rhythm as he struck by guess in the dark, and then, snatching hastily at his bundle of dynamite, he thrust the sticks into the hole. He laid on more powder, making some mud with his canteen water and plastering it over the charge, but, as he drew out the fuse and split it for lighting, he paused and looked about.

"Here," he said, rising abruptly from his place and laying a short length of fuse in Whittle's hand, "that's your torch . . . light it first, and, if anything happens, touch off the fuse and beat it down the gulch."

He caught up his drills and moved away through the shadows, and soon, from the other bridge base, Whittle heard the *clink* of his hammer. It sounded loudly, very loudly, and it dragged on endlessly, and then, from the bridge above them, a man's voice shouted out. A silence fell and still another voice took up the cry—the sentinels were calling the hour.

"*¡La o-ocha!*" droned Bogan in the person of the missing guard. "*¡Sentinel alerta!*"

As no corporal of the guard appeared, he went boldly on with his work. Hours passed—or so it seemed, although no hours were called—and, at last, with his tools in a sack, Beanie came sneaking back to the horses.

"All right, now," he said, "I got her drilled deep and loaded to the muzzle with straight nitro. You light yours first, and, when you see mine flash up, mount your horse and drift down the gulch. Are you ready?"

"Yes . . . no!" answered Whittle. "What about this sentinel? We can't leave him here to be killed."

"Huh? One Mexican, more or less," grunted Bogan contemptuously, but after a moment's thought he stopped and picked the man up. "Hold that pack horse," he muttered, "but, whatever happens, don't forget to light your fuse." There was a scuffle as he heaved up the battered Mexican and the pack horse snorted and shied. "Let 'im go!" commanded Bogan abruptly, dropping the man as a sentinel challenged from above. "¡Váyese!" he returned in the person of the felled sentry and added an obscene epithet to make the verisimilitude complete. Then he jogged Whittle with his elbow and, swift as a weasel, slipped across to fire his hole. On the abutment above them the sentry stood watching, still doubtful as to what was going on, and Whittle knelt down by his fuse. In the shelter of his hat he struck a match and touched it quickly to his torch. A flame spouted out, and, at a yell from above, he applied it swiftly to the fuse. There was a flare of light, the horses flew back, and, as he turned and clutched at the lariat, the fuse like a writhing serpent began to sputter toward its charge.

"Come on," hissed Bogan almost knocking him over as he rushed up and grabbed his mount, and then the sentry opened fire. Instantly all was confusion, with horses struggling and Beanie cursing like mad, until out of the thick of it he dashed down the cañon, with the pack animal trailing behind. Whittle's horse broke to follow. He missed catching his stirrup, and then he felt his foot on the sentry. He was lying, helpless, where Bogan had flung him— but should they leave him there to die? Whittle stooped down swiftly and caught him in his arms, and, as his horse raced away down the gulch, he followed on foot with the Mexican across his shoulders. In that moment of decision he had chosen to save the sentinel, but, as he staggered around the point, he met Beanie coming back with his mount.

"Put down that man!" Bogan commanded hoarsely, and flung the Mexican into the brush. "He's safe." He cursed. "A damned sight safer than you are. Now git on your horse and ride!"

Whittle rode, and, as they whirled on down the tortuous cañon, their horses lunged at a thunderous shock. The sky flashed up yellow, and, as the explosion rent the air, the earth rocked with a second great blast.

"Wait! Listen!" exclaimed Bogan, reining his horse in cruelly, and at the crash of falling girders he laughed. "She's down!" he exulted. "The damned, chile-eating greasers . . . they won't mend that bridge in a month. Now up the track we go, halfway to Fronteras, and burn every trestle we come across."

He let out his horse and set off at a gallop with Whittle following closely at his heels. They cleared the cañon and swung sharply to the north, whirling out across the plains with the wind hurrying them on from behind. It seemed to Whittle as if they traveled on the storm, with the yuccas slipping by like ghosts. Then abruptly Bogan reined his horse to the east and rode up a sheltered gulch.

"Here's a trestle," he said, staring intently through the darkness, and after a moment, with a can of coal oil, he ventured up to the bridge.

A half an hour later as they looked behind them they could see a tongue of flame against the sky. It was the sign of the bridge burner, making evident to everyone their handiwork and where they were. Yet, despite the danger, Beanie galloped forward recklessly and set fire to bridge after bridge. A very devil of destruction seemed to take possession of him, whirling him on through the teeth of the storm, and, when at a cañon bridge the startled sentries fired at him, he charged with a yell that routed them. Straight along the track, with a great glare behind him, he spurred on till his horse hung its head, and then, reluctantly, he turned off into the hills to seek a safe hiding place from pursuit.

They were far to the north of that low range of mountains at whose base they had blown up the bridge yet still far south of the high, jagged Sierras that offered Montaño's army its retreat. The country was level with rolling sandhills and broad, hard-packed alkali flats, and, before the sun rose and set on their burned bridges, there would be vengeful loyalists in pursuit. With their horses deadbeat, Beanie plowed on at a walk, following a cow trail that led to a sunken gulch where a pool of bitter water lay cupped. They rested a while, rubbing down their spent animals, and once more Beanie mounted and spurred on. For three careful nights he had traveled by some instinct that took him to cover at dawn, but now in the wind and darkness they drifted like lost cattle before a storm.

At the first flush of daylight, Beanie rode for the summit of a knoll, but the false dawn faded and the plain was obscured again before they could look out over it. Then the gray dawn followed, creeping coldly from the east where their ravished railroad lay, and, as the darkness passed, suddenly Bogan ripped out an oath and jerked his wearied horses out of sight.

"Holy, jumping Jehu!" he sputtered, snatching his field glasses out of the case, and with Whittle beside him he crept back to the summit and looked down the other side. Not a mile away lay the railroad itself, its poles rising like sentinels against the dawn, and along the track a long train of cattle cars was giving out horses and men. It was a squadron of cavalry and a yell from the scouts showed that already their presence was known.

"It's a troop train from Fronteras!" burst out Beanie in a panic. "Where in Hades is that army of Montaño's? Here I do my part and cut off Chulita and they let the whole garrison come down on me! So help me Gawd, if I get out of this alive, I'll never trust a Mexican again."

A bugle sounded, but he turned his back on them to search out the country behind.

"No use," he said, "our horses are dead. We could never make a ride to those hills."

"Then what can we do?" asked Whittle at last as Beanie focused his glasses on the flat plains, and Bogan glared at him with bloodshot, angry eyes.

"We can get into that sinkhole," he said, pointing at a gash on the flat, "and try to stand 'em off."

He ran back to his horse and, shaking him up with lash and spurs, rushed him off violently down the slope. As Whittle followed, he saw the Federal scouts riding hard to cut them off. They were betrayed then by Montaño and the military Gambolier, after all their solemn assurances. The appointed day had come and they had dynamited the bridges, but Montaño had not surrounded Fronteras. He had waited like a Mexican, and now the federal cavalry had been rushed down to wipe them out. Perchance Montaño was still in camp with his dilatory leaders or gazing at Fronteras from afar, or perhaps Gambolier, for military reasons, had purposely left the railroad uncut. For, to catch two bridge burners, the commander at Fronteras had sent down over 200 men, and, with them out of town, it would be so much the easier to beat down the garrison that was left. There was some reason, of course, but as Whittle fled before the scouts, he felt again the injustice of life. He was a pawn in the game, a victim, in every circumstance, and now, after losing his beloved to Pedley, he was offered as a sacrifice to Montaño. Yet, if that was his doom, he could at least sell his life dearly as a last, futile protest against his fate.

The sinkhole they rode for was a mere gash in the broad flat, where the baked earth was checked like a crack in an apple and revealed the brackish water beneath. To drink at the hole the wild range cattle had worn trails that led like winding streamers across the plain and at the tank itself they had plowed great trenches down the bank to the muddied pool. As he plunged down the slope with the bullets flying about him, Whittle found Bogan all unsaddled and his horses thrown and tied.

"Here, fill them with dirt," he said, throwing Whittle some empty gunny sacks, and then, with his eyes on the circling scouts, he put his shoulder against Whittle's horse and threw him, with one heave, on his side. A bugle blew the charge, and, on the far line of sandhills, a troop of flying cavalry appeared, but at a shot from Beanie they wheeled abruptly and disappeared over the summit of the hill. Once more the bugle blew, and, deployed now as skirmishers, the well-trained troopers dashed forth. Down the slope they came in a cloud of dust, with guidons flying at left and right, and behind his sandbags Beanie eyed them grimly as he talked from the corner of his mouth.

"Well, here they come," he said. "Get your gun and come over here. They may get away with it, but I'm going to knock down them guidons, the first two shots I unhook. I'm an expert rifleman, if you know what that means, the highest grade of sharpshooter there is. I can hit 'em in the head as far as I can see 'em . . . that's why they call me Beanie Bogan. I got that in the islands, shooting goo-goos out of palm trees, but I didn't have this damned wind to fight. Now all you do is load . . . don't you fire a shot . . . just pass me your rifle and refill the magazine of mine. By grab, we may croak, but, before we do it, I'll make Mexican the court language of hell."

He set his jaw and drew a bead on the sergeant who was galloping with the gun to the right. Twice he caught his breath but the distance was too great—he wanted the shot to count. In a great semicircle the flying squadron came charging down on their hole, and then Beanie's gun spoke out. Horse and man went down, and the guidon with them, and Bogan jerked viciously at his lever. Then his gun barrel swung swiftly to the other guidon, and he fired three shots against the wind. The first two missed, but, as the third rang out, the guidon bearer tumbled to the ground. *Bang, bang* rattled the rifle, and, as horses and men went down, Bogan reached over and snatched the loaded gun. Whittle ejected the last empty and stuffed the magazine with cartridges, and once more Bogan grabbed the gun. The tattoo of his gunfire was timed now to a rhythm, fast at first but lagging to slow shots, and, as it ceased abruptly, Whittle looked over the edge while Bogan let out a yell. Where the trim columns had been, each trooper in his place, galloping confidently down to surround them, there was now a rout of disorganized horsemen, turned back by the fire of one man.

"Here's for luck!" Bogan exulted, and, aiming long, he knocked a last trooper from his saddle. They waited then, and, as the squadron disappeared, Bogan rose up and looked around.

"Well," he said, "that'll hold 'em till sundown, and then you'll have your wish."

"What wish?" asked Whittle, and Bogan smiled grimly as he breathed through the barrel of his rifle.

"Why," he said, "they'll sneak up and pot us . . . a Mex can shoot as good as I can, after dark."

CHAPTER SEVEN

An hour wore on miserably, and, beating up against the wind, a pair of ravens came over from the distant mountains to hover above the unburied dead. Bogan became moody and irritable, Whittle despondent and oblivious, and, as the morning passed and even the scouts disappeared, they slept, turn about, in the dirt. At last the sun set, and, rousing up from his apathy, Beanie once more took command. The horses were released from their bonds and saddled, the pack was reduced to almost nothing, and, as the darkness gathered and no Mexicans appeared, Bogan slipped away down the draw. Sometime that night, when they least expected it, their enemies would come tumbling into their hole, and then, of course, there would be nothing to it but a running fight in the dark. So they waited, worn and nerve-racked, until at last Bogan came back and stripped the pack horse of his load.

"Let's get action," he said, and, lashing the animal cruelly with his quirt, he sent him at a gallop across the plain. The wind had gone down and they could hear him clearly as he clattered along over the flat, but no guns spit fire, no lurking troopers charged, nothing checked him as he raced away.

"Well, what's the answer?" demanded Bogan, and then, loading out his horse, he tightened the girth and mounted. "I'm tired of this," he said. "Do you want to make a run for it?"

Whittle followed willingly behind. He had no nerves now, no fears, no hopes, just a wearied acceptance of his fate. They rode out slowly, heading for the mountains to the west, but nowhere about them in the echoing darkness could they see a single movement of life. They rode a mile across the barren flat, and, as his horse found some bunch grass by a sandhill, Bogan stopped and let him eat.

"Don't see nothing," he muttered as Whittle came alongside, and, while their famished animals grazed, they sat in silence and listened for the sound of pursuit. "Well, let's take a chance," said Bogan at last, and, reining up his mount, he spurred him into action and went dashing away toward the hills. They gained them, unchallenged, and at the entrance to a cañon Bogan turned in his saddle and cursed.

"Well, damn a Mexican!" he burst out incredulously. "Where in Hades do you think they are?"

"They all went back to the train," answered Whittle at last, "this morning, when the bugle gave the call."

"All right, then," boasted Bogan, "according to that, I cleaned the whole outfit. You have to hand it to me. And yet," he added, "it ain't like them Federals . . . they could have got us like shooting fish." He rode up the draw where the bunch grass grew rankly and dismounted to let his horse feed, but still he muttered on to himself: "It ain't right. There's some trick here somewhere . . . they don't let no bridge burners get away."

They rode up the valley, and then into a narrow cañon, and on until the trail forked at the divide, and the cold dawn found them far up in the mountains without a single soldier in pursuit. "I got it!" cried Beanie when he realized his good fortune. "Montaño has made his raid on Fronteras!"

That was his last word on the enigma with which he had wrestled all night, and Whittle had no theory to advance. All they knew was that the cavalry, which had surprised them in such numbers, had disappeared as suddenly as it had come, and three days later, when they rode into their old camp, they found Beanie's guess was good. Montaño's soldiers were gone, their campfires were dead, and the tracks all pointed toward Fronteras.

"Why, the lazy Mexican bastards!" cried Bogan in a passion when he perceived that the tracks were still fresh, "they ain't been gone two days. We had about one chance in a hundred thousand of getting out of that jackpot alive, and here Montaño and his pot-licking greasers have been bumming around camp all the time. You wait till I find 'im. I don't care what he says. I don't care if he's taken the town. I'm going to cuss him out for a palavering coward, and then I'm going to quit him. I won't work for no man that'll lie to me like that. Can't you see it sticking out? Well, it's easy for me ... they don't want to let go of that ten thousand! Yes, certainly!" he exploded. "I *know* that's why they did it. It's just some more of Gambolier's strategy! We go down there first and burn all the bridges ... that cuts off the troops from Chulita ... and then, by grab, they let the cavalry go down after us, and that cuts off two hundred more. *And* ... by getting us killed, that saves the ten thousand dollars and they win, both ways from the jack. That's the way they do all of us Americans ... they work us for suckers ... but you watch 'em when I stage my comeback. They'll be surprised, and, take it from me, they won't dare to look me in the eye. A man can't do it. If he's plotted to murder you, he can't look you straight in the eye."

The journey toward Fronteras was filled with threats and mutterings, for Beanie was in a villainous mood. On their long ride north they had encountered few houses, and those of the poorest class. Bogan's stomach had turned against jerked beef. Yet, so poor and miserable were the mountain dwellers, that they could offer them little else. Now, as they rode in on their half-starved mounts, with the strain on their tense nerves let down, they paid without knowing it for those nights of excitement when they had burned the Central bridges. They were nervous and twitchy, impatient over trifles, and torn by contending moods. As they encountered a camp of Montaño's soldiers at the head of the narrow cañon, they passed them without a word.

The Army of Liberation was encamped in a brushy valley that led up from the Río Grande, and, as Bogan saw visitors from the American side moving about among the fires, he exploded in heartfelt oaths. If it had been a *fiesta* on the streets of Fronteras, there could not have been more tourists with cameras. There were no outposts, no guards, no signs of army discipline, but each *insurrecto* band was camped by itself as if there were no enemy for miles. Guns and equipment lay everywhere. Men rode about at will, and in the midst of it all—the smoldering fires, the bright serapes, the big-hatted mountaineer Mexicans—there eddied a throng of sightseers from Del Norte, distributing tobacco and food to the men. As the two haggard men came out of the box cañon and rode down through this assembly, Beanie Bogan became the object of all eyes. He was gaunt and bearded, with unwashed features, and his clothes torn and stained with dirt. Behind him, no less travel-worn, rode the wraith of the man Whittle, who had stood off the *rurales* with a shotgun.

He was changed now from the immaculate Whittle, who had done his first fighting in decent black. The sad eyes that had once been so gentle were bloodshot and defiant, his clean shoulders were bowed with fatigue, and, as he followed after Beanie, he bore a certain likeness to that ruthless master of men. The wild life was telling on him; he had been harried and hunted, and now suddenly he was a fighting animal. Men gazed at him in silence, as they did at Espinoso and others of

Montaño's famous outlaws, and the women drew together as he passed. Whittle was aware, without knowing the cause, that he was suddenly set apart from other men. He was a bridge burner, a wrecker, a soldier of fortune, the partner of the fighting Beanie Bogan.

They found the Foreign Legion encamped near the river, in full view of the other side, and, as they rode on toward the whitewashed adobe, before which Montaño stood receiving his friends, they were greeted by an American cheer. It came from Big Bill McCafferty, and Jimmy Sullivan, the deserter, and hulking Helge Wahlgren, and from twenty more grinning recruits.

"Three cheers for Beanie Bogan!" shouted Big Bill with unction, but Beanie regarded him coldly.

"Hello, you big stiff!" he responded with a sneer. "What are you fellers doing up here?"

"We're preparing to attack Fronteras!" replied Sullivan joyously. "What's the matter, Beanie? You look kinder sick."

"Yes, and I feel kinder sick," returned Bogan sarcastically. "What have we got here . . . a Sunday school picnic?"

"Well, it's Sunday," admitted Sullivan, "if that's what you mean. But we're waiting for further reinforcements."

"Ain't surrounded the town yet, eh?" inquired Bogan shortly, and spurred through the crowd toward Montaño.

"Ah, my friend!" cried Montaño in an ecstasy of excitement when he recognized Bogan beneath his beard, and ran and caught him in his arms.

"Yes, like hell!" returned Bogan, releasing himself impatiently. "Something like your other friend, Buck O'Donnell!"

"Buck O'Donnell?" repeated Montaño, raising his eyebrows inquiringly.

"Yes," answered Beanie with brutal directness, "only this friend didn't happen to get killed!"

He tapped himself on the breast, which heaved with sudden anger, and then he burst into a tirade. The crowd became larger, newspaper reporters fought their way forward, while Montaño strove in vain to check him.

"Just a moment!" he protested. "Only listen, my dear Bo-gan. Come inside . . . it can all be explained."

"Yes, sure it can be explained," agreed Bogan profanely, "but would that bring me back to life? I can explain to you why Buck O'Donnell got killed . . . and tell you whose fault it was, too."

"Come inside . . . and bring your friend," suggested Montaño quietly, and they followed him into an inner room.

It was a plain adobe house with dirt floors and rawhide furniture, but in this, the inner sanctuary, there was a great table strewn with maps. On the opposite side of it, immersed in some problem, sat Gambolier, the military adviser. He rose up slowly and regarded them questioningly, and to the excited Beanie his aloofness was proof enough of guilt.

"No, I won't shake hands," he grumbled morosely as Gambolier stepped forward to congratulate him. "I came here to get my money."

"What money?" demanded Gambolier, and Bogan rushed at him threateningly and wagged his finger in his face.

"You know what money!" he shouted accusingly. "The ten thousand dollars that was coming to us if we went down and blew up that bridge. Well, we blowed her up, and we burned a lot of trestles, and, now by the Lord, we want our money . . . and we're going to get it, too!"

He added this confidently, turning his keen eyes upon Montaño who had ventured once more to intervene.

"Yes, yes, my dear Bo-gan," he protested smilingly, "but don't make a scene with Gambolier. The agreement was with me, and you shall have the money, so sit down and make your report."

"I've made my report," answered Beanie sharply. "The Arroyo Grande bridge is a total wreck and we burned seven trestles coming north. And then, by grab, when we'd scrapped the whole railroad and rode our horses to a standstill, we come over a hill and here's a whole troop train of cavalry that's been sent down from Fronteras to take us. Now you can explain that all you want to, but there's nothing talks to me like ten thousand dollars . . . in my hand."

He held out his hand and patted it dramatically, but Montaño still smiled at him tolerantly.

"Ah, yes," he said, "you shall have the money. It is still there, in escrow, at the bank. When the two weeks are up, if no trains cross the bridge, you shall have it, without a doubt. We are very sorry about that matter of the cavalry, but. . . ."

"It was a military necessity," explained Gambolier suavely, and Beanie Bogan nodded sneeringly.

"Yes," he said, "I was listening for that."

"It was, indeed!" exclaimed Gambolier warmly. "It was impracticable to surround the town."

"But what about me?" inquired Bogan meaningly. "Where did I get off, in your military calculations? It was distinctly agreed before I started out that on the Twentieth of April I was to blow up the bridges and you was to surround Fronteras. But you've got three thousand men, camped up here in the cañon, and you don't seem to have surrounded it yet."

"Ah, but you don't understand," cried Gambolier excitedly, "we have no effective artillery!"

"No, and I don't want to understand," answered Bogan roughly. "I've quit, and I've come for my pay."

"Oh, no!" burst out Montaño, and rushed to restrain him, but Beanie jerked violently away.

"It's a wonder," he suggested, "that someone don't ask me how I come to get away from that cavalry."

"Well, how did you?" flattered Montaño, patting him affectionately on the shoulder. "By some foxy trick?"

"No, I whipped 'em, by God!" responded Bogan proudly. "And youse guys are afraid to surround Fronteras."

He put a world of scorn into the lash of those words, and Montaño shrank back as from a whip.

"Perhaps we were waiting," he suggested coldly,

"for you to come back and show us how."

"Well, I'm back," replied Bogan, "and I could show you how. But it would be easier to recruit a hundred fighting Irish and go in and do it myself."

"You are confident," observed Gambolier with a thin-lipped smile, and Montaño ventured a scornful shrug.

"I'm a soldier," returned Beanie stoutly, "and fighting is my business. But how about that ten thousand dollars?"

"It is in the bank," answered Montaño stiffly. "You will receive it when the two weeks are up."

"No, I'll receive it now. Just write me out an order before I begin to get rough."

Bogan's beady terrier eyes glowed red from beneath his eyebrows, and, as silence fell upon the room, he fingered his pistol suggestively.

"Very well," spoke up Montaño, but, as he shook out his fountain pen, he gave way to a sigh of bitterness. "Very well, Sergeant Bo-gan, but, according to our agreement. . . ."

"Our agreement? You broke it first! You was to protect me by surrounding Fronteras!"

"You were to wait till the two weeks were up. What assurance have we that the bridge is destroyed? None at all but your own unsupported word."

"My word is good," observed Bogan as he slipped the check into his pocket, "and I'll give you a little advice before I go. You better get you another military adviser."

He stuck out his chin at Gambolier and started for the door, but Montaño ran hastily after him.

"Just a moment, Sergeant Bo-gan," he implored in a whisper. "Would you consider . . . bringing over some big guns?"

"Nothing doing," answered Bogan, but his steps lagged a little, and at the outer door he stopped. "I'll tell you," he said. "We'll see if this check's good first."

And with a leering grin he was gone.

Chapter Eight

On their return to Del Norte, as on his departure, Bruce Whittle was no more than a sad-eyed automaton, a patient shadow of Beanie Bogan. He followed him silently across the swaying suspension bridge and past the rigid and oblivious soldier who stood guard at the American side. He followed him into the closed and waiting automobile that had appeared so mysteriously to receive them, and with the admiring murmurs of the crowd in his ears he went flying with Beanie into town. It was all a part of the terrifying death machine to which he had committed his poor self and that, after whirling him through the wilds of Chihuahua and back through a phantasmagoria of flight, now spewed him out, at the end of the journey, safe as a child who has dared the shoot-the-chutes.

He had gone out to die, but now that he had escaped, his mind was purged of petty hopes and fears, and he gave no thought to what was going on. If the people stared and pointed, if the barber refused his fee, or high officials smiled wisely and shook hands, it was no more personal to him than the very evident fact that Del Norte had gone war mad. The city was crowded with transcontinental tourists who had taken stopovers to wait for the big fight. The barrooms were jammed with old soldiers and frontier characters, making prophecies on the date of the battle, and at every place he went, still in the shadow of Beanie Bogan, he found himself lauded as a hero.

The news of the dynamiting of the Central bridges had set the whole city in an uproar, and then, hot upon it, had come the word that Montaño was marching upon Fronteras. He had come, and, the moment his high-hatted *insurrectos* appeared, Del Norte went wild with excitement. After lurking for months in the mountains of Chihuahua, recruiting peons, raiding ranches, and attacking towns, Montaño, the mastermind of the ever-spreading revolution, had come out into the open to fight. It would be a spectacle that men would always speak of, the attack on the stronghold of Fronteras—within the town the trained Federals of Reyes, fully equipped with artillery and machine-guns, without the swarming hosts of half-savage *insurrectos*, clothed in rags and inspired with the high valor of patriots.

A host of correspondents and special writers descended upon Del Norte overnight and, as the Army of Liberation, dirty, hungry, and out of tobacco, came boldly down to the river, they were overwhelmed and astounded by the onrush of visitors and by the gifts that followed in their wake. In a day there was tobacco for every insurgent, and presents of food and clothes. Peace officers and government officials felt the influence of public opinion and winked at the violations of neutrality, and suddenly, in a great burst of popular enthusiasm, every man became a partisan of Montaño.

But the great battle had not materialized. Fronteras was not surrounded, and, although the Foreign Legion had been doubled in a week by a rush of adventurous Americans, Montaño had done nothing but delay. Hence the riotous welcome to Beanie Bogan and his bridge-burning partner, Whittle—the man who never talked.

It was in the lounge of the exclusive The Cholla, where with Bogan he had retired to escape the attention of the crowd, that Bruce Whittle suddenly woke to his old life. For two weeks he had moved in a waking dream, responding quickly to every reaction but wrapped in a blessed oblivion. The sharp agony of his loss had produced its own anodyne, and he was drugged by the contemplation of sudden death, but now in a moment, as a face appeared before him, the curtain of Nepenthe was torn. While Beanie, always the center of interest, was replying in guarded sentences to the jovial accusations of his friends, a man peered in through the door. His eyes met Whittle's, then were quickly averted, and in a moment Broughton Pedley was gone. Then the old memories rushed back, and Whittle sat, tense and staring, while slowly, as if moved by some ponderous mechanism, a wedding scene passed before his eyes.

He saw the bridal hall, the decorated chancel, the huddle of silent guests, and then, down the stairway, she came again, Constance, the woman that he loved. Once more she met his glance, then moved on to the chancel and the old irresolution came over him. He heard the words of the ceremony, hurried forward so precipitately; he heard her answer, and Pedley's, and then the end. Again he woke to the feeling of horror, to the sense that he had lost her forever, and, too late, he roused up from his trance. He was brave, now that it was too late; his strength could move mountains, but what was there now to win? Nothing but a kiss, to remember always, to cherish to the end of his days. He moved forward with the rest, he met her, she rushed to his arms, and then—the kiss.

It changed now and mingled, the slow-moving vision that had been burning on the tissues of his brain, but always it came back, that appeal in her eyes as she gazed after him and called him by name. She had called him Bruce, and ever since in his dreams he had thought of her as Constance. And she loved him still, although she had suffered the martyrdom of marriage with Broughton Pedley, and, he knew this, too—she would always love him and remain faithful to his memory. She was there, in Del Norte, and he had come back as from the dead, perhaps—well, perhaps, he might see her once more.

Whittle had never forgotten the well meaning arguments with which Beanie had attacked his resolve, and it did seem unreasonable, since she wished to see him, to deny her that moment of grace. It would be painful, for when he looked at her now, she was not Constance, she was Pedley's wife—but if it would make her any happier in the years to come, he must go through with it for her sake. And she would be watching for him now, she would read in the papers of his desperate adventures in Mexico, and would know that he had sought death for her.

He rose up suddenly as a twisted bit of paper was thrust into his hand from behind, but, although he turned quickly, he saw only a call boy, slipping deftly away through the crowd. Beanie had not seen it; he was busy telling stories, and Whittle glanced at the hasty note. It was written awkwardly in a cramped, left-handed fashion that was obviously intended to disguise, but at the bottom was signed her name.

Am watched but must see you. Follow man at the door.

Constance

Whittle glanced over at Beanie then. When his attention was diverted, he rose and started for the door. But, despite his preoccupation, Beanie had not missed the proceedings and he grabbed him as he passed down the hall.

"Here," he said, "what's the big idea? Don't you know you're liable to get pinched? Your name's in the paper . . . you're alleged to be a dynamiter . . . but you're safe inside that door."

"I . . . I was just going out for a little walk," began Whittle lamely, but Bogan was not to be deceived.

"Nothing doing," he declared. "You stay right here by me. If you don't, you'll get into trouble."

"But I don't like it in here," answered Whittle fretfully. "I want to get some fresh air."

"Well, it ain't fresh, believe me," returned Bogan fervently, "the kind they have in the jail. I broke in there once, before I learned my business."

"Well, I'm going anyhow," broke in Whittle sharply, and Bogan's lip curled in a smile.

"All right," he said, "give 'er my regards . . . and send for me, when you land on your ear."

"You mind your own business," flashed back Whittle, and whipped out the massive door.

It was dusk, almost dark, but, as he stepped into the street, a man appeared from a sheltering archway and beckoned him to follow. He was not a man that Whittle had seen before and yet in some way he seemed familiar. There was something about the set of his heavy neck and the way he planted his feet, and he was leading him down toward the river. The streets became narrower and the houses lower, and, at a bridge across the canal, Whittle stopped. Below the canal, as he knew very well, lay Chihuahua town and the mud huts of the Mexicans. It was none too safe even in the middle of the day and—what would Constance be doing there?

"Come on!" called the man, and, as Whittle shook his head, he turned back impatiently to join him. "Say, listen," he said, "I'm a private detective in the employ of a certain lady. My client wants to see you. . . ."

"She isn't down there," answered Whittle with decision. "Perhaps you've got the wrong man."

"Ain't you Mister Whittle?" demanded the detective, coming closer. "Didn't you get her note at

The Cholla? Well, come on, then. She's crazy to see you. She said you was just to have faith."

"Well, where is she?" questioned Whittle, following after him reluctantly. "There's nothing but Mexicans down here."

"I'll tell you," whispered the detective, speaking hoarsely in his ear, "she come down here to hide from her . . . husband."

He gave him a playful dig with his elbow and strode on toward a lighted house, but at the entrance Whittle halted irresolutely. The house stood by itself, on the edge of the river, and it had a sinister air. He recalled of a sudden the warnings of Beanie, and that other affair with a detective. "Step in, sir," said the detective, still holding the door open, "you'll find her just inside."

"Well . . . ask her to come out," suggested Whittle at last, and then suddenly the man's attitude changed.

"Say," he blustered, "you're going in that door or I'll know the reason why. Now . . . are you coming, or must I throw you in?" He stepped out swiftly, as if to cut off Whittle's retreat, and then he spoke more quietly. "You don't need to be afraid, but she offered me a reward of several hundred dollars, and I'm sure going to deliver the goods."

He moved forward ponderously, and, after facing him a moment, Whittle turned and stepped through the door. What did it matter to him if the detective was lying? If she wished to see him, she would have to engage some messenger, and detectives were much of a kind. The fact that this ruffian imputed a dishonorable motive to her note and his instant response to it should not bar the way to those few precious moments that he must snatch before he went back to die. And if he was deceived—well, what did it matter? What did anything matter, after all?

He entered the room doubtfully, and a candle on the table guttered low before the draft of air, but when the puny flame threw its light into the shadows, he saw Broughton Pedley, smiling.

"Well," he said as he stepped out from his hiding place, "so I've caught you at last."

"Yes," answered Whittle, but, although he said it quietly, his chest began to heave with excitement. The sight of this man, who he had so scrupulously avoided, released a gust of fierce passions in his breast, and, as he noticed the smile, his lips began to tremble and his hands clutched and worked with rage. "Yes," he said, "but you may live to regret it. You may wish you had let me alone. I warn you now. . . ."

"Oh, you warn *me?*" taunted Pedley, and then he laughed unpleasantly. "I may as well tell you that I've got you dead to rights." He raised his hand, and, from a darkened doorway, two men emerged with pistols drawn.

"Just search him for arms," ordered Pedley confidently, and Whittle submitted in a daze. "And now step outside," continued Pedley to his men. "I'd like to talk with this gentleman alone."

The door closed behind them, and, as Whittle stood waiting, Pedley paced up and down the room. "Mister Whittle," he began at last, "you have made me a lot of trouble and I feel justified in using strong-arm methods. In fact, the way things have come about, I am greatly tempted to dispose of you. But I will give you another chance, in order not to disturb my wife."

He paused, and, as Whittle winced at the word, he looked him in the eyes,

"Yes, my wife," he repeated. "I have sworn to love, cherish, and protect her, and, before God, I will keep my promise. If you won't listen to reason, if you won't go out of her life and promise never to return, I'll throw you into that river with as little compunction as I would the body of a dog. I know who you are . . . a cowardly blackmailer . . . but you can't work your game with me. I might, if I were easy, offer you a certain amount of money to give up your designs on my home, but there are other methods, and I have chosen to employ them. Now . . . here's the way matters stand."

He folded his arms and regarded Whittle sternly while he went on with portentous calm.

"By rights I should take you across the river and deliver you to the Federal commander. There is a standing reward for your apprehension, and the penalty of your crime is death. But if you will sign this paper . . . which simply states the truth, that you were only trying to marry her for her money. . . ."

"I was not!" denied Whittle in a white heat of anger. "You lie, you dirty crook! You have no understanding of honor. If you were only a gentleman, you might know that my motives. . . ."

"Didn't you come here tonight," broke in Pedley accusingly, "in response to a fake note from her? Didn't you come sneaking down here, thinking you would meet her alone? And didn't you

know that she was my wife? Well, no wonder you
are ashamed. I think, under the circumstances,
that I have behaved very handsomely in not resorting to absolute violence."

"Well, I did come," admitted Whittle at last,
"but I thought she might need my aid. She's unhappy . . . I know it . . . and I'd give my right
hand. . . ."

"Not necessary," answered Pedley glibly. "Just
sign your name to this statement."

He whipped out a paper and spread it on the
table while he held out a fountain pen—but Whittle struck it out of his hand.

"You poor, ignorant, fool," he hissed through his
teeth, "do you think I'd sign anything for you?"

"You will," threatened Pedley, "or be dragged
across the river to be executed as a self-confessed
dynamiter. Now, you can take your choice, but
I've notified the commander and he'll. . . ."

"Go ahead," challenged, Whittle. "If you think
you can do it, just put me across the river. No,
you . . . *you* . . . !" He rushed at him impetuously
as Pedley called for help and they went down together on the floor.

"Help! Help!" cried Pedley, and an instinctive
loathing made Whittle's fingers close on his
throat. He hated the very touch of his plump,
yielding body, the gasp of his breath against his
cheek, and he shook him as a dog shakes a snake.
They rose up struggling, the table crashed beneath
them, and, as they went down again in the darkness, Whittle struck him with all his strength in
the face. Rough hands laid hold upon him and
wrenched him away, but the old, animal hatred,

the primordial savagery that bade him kill the man who had stolen his mate, rose up in an instant and he jerked himself free while he aimed one more blow at his enemy. He struck out indiscriminately, for they were all against him until, in the darkness a pistol, swung at random, caught him fairly across the head. He went down, half stunned, and in the silence that followed the babble of Spanish smote his ears. A crowd of Mexicans was gathered about the doorway, gazing in but afraid to enter, until suddenly a fat man, bearing a lantern and a pistol, came striding into the room.

"*¿Quién viva?*" he demanded, throwing his lantern upon their faces, and at sight of Whittle he stopped. "Ah! My frien'!" he cried, and, looking up from the ground, Whittle recognized the purple visage of Rico. "My frien'!" he cried again, and, raising his pistol vindictively, he felled a burly detective to the floor. "*¡Socorro, amigos!*" he shouted to his friends. "*¡Socorro, amigos, y viva* Montaño!"

"*¡Viva* Montaño!" yelled the crowd, and with a savage rush they came tumbling in through the door.

"Hah, my frien'!" exclaimed Rico, dragging Whittle to a corner and protecting him with his body from the rout, "I have save your life . . . like mine!"

CHAPTER NINE

With Rico to the fore the chances were small that Whittle would be delivered to the Federals. Although the Mexican was a drunken brute, with a black record as a smuggler, ingratitude could not be charged up against him, and so great was his anger at the assailants of his friend that he flew at them again in a fury. The crowd followed suit, for in Little Chihuahua Rico Puga was an uncrowned king, and the combat assumed the proportions of a riot until, at a signal, the mob rushed away, carrying Whittle bodily in their midst.

"No be afraid," panted Rico in his ear, "officers come . . . no want a fight."

The darkness behind them was punctuated by pistol shots as the officers discharged their guns in the air, and the hurried *slap* of brogans marked the precipitate flight of most of Rico's mob, but enough remained to carry Whittle to the *fonda* and hide him in an upstairs room. There, while Rico stayed below and stoutly asserted that he had no knowledge of the riot, an old woman bathed the cut on Whittle's head and bound it up in a clean rag. Then, as the excitement subsided and the officers left the quarter, Rico scurried up the stairs to get the news.

"What they fight you for?" he demanded eagerly as a bevy of staring Mexicans appeared behind. "You smuggle guns? You start one scrap? Them men work for Porfilio Reyes?"

"No, they're private detectives," answered Whittle unwillingly, "but they were going to deliver me to Reyes."

"Ah, I weesh I had keel them!" exclaimed Rico fiercely. "What for they want to ketch you?"

"Well," began Whittle, and then he hesitated, for Beanie had warned him not to talk. "They said there was a reward on my head."

"On your head? Oh, to geet you. But what for, my frien', what for?"

"Never mind. Well . . . for burning bridges."

A great light came into Rico's staring eyes as he rolled them wisely at the crowd. "But you ain't burn them bridges, hey?" he questioned, laughing heartily. "Hah, my frien', we understand all that, and, when you have troble, when them bad mans try ketch you, you come to my house, understan'?" He made some remark to the Mexicans behind him, and they turned and tramped down the stairs. "By gol," he went on, flashing his teeth at Whittle, "I hear all about that bridge. And my frien', Beanie Bo-gan, he is sure one brave man, but Montaño, I don' know. Why don't he march up and battle Fronteras? All them people been move out, maybe one week, maybe two. They don't like be in that town, but now pretty soon they all go back ... they go home, to keep bad men from steal."

The sorrows of the poor people of Fronteras who had so accommodatingly crossed over to Del Norte to allow Montaño to take their town were very near to Rico's heart, but as he was still in the midst of an account of their flight, there was a step on the stairway below.

"Hah! Bo-gan!" cried Rico, but as he rushed to welcome him, Beanie shoved him rudely aside.

"Hey! Come on!" he said to Whittle. "Your friend has turned out the guard."

"What?" demanded Whittle, rising up from his couch, "are the detectives out after us again?"

"And the soldiers," answered Bogan as he hustled him down, the stairs. "They've given orders to prevent us from crossing. Your friend came uptown with his nose on his cheek, looking like a pound and a half of rump steak, and the first men he run into was the United States marshal and the captain of the provost guard. Then he made a big holler about how you had beat him and turned him over to a mob of Montañistas, and, of course, the marshal and the captain sent out word to have you arrested. But I'll get you across ... large bodies move slowly, and we'll beat the captain's orders to the dam ... but, oh, my boy, you're a vindikitive cuss. Now come on up the track ... and take off that rag or you'll never get by in the world. But, oh, lawzee, I'm never going to speak cross to you again, the way you chopped up Pedley. I seen it in your eye, when you left The Cholla, but I never looked for nothing like this."

He set off up the track at a long soldier's trot, still murmuring his admiration and awe, and Whittle let it pass in grim silence. It was nothing to him what Bogan believed or disbelieved, and nothing mattered now—he had lost. But Beanie was so pleased at his supposed act of vengeance that, even after they had started across the dam, he turned back to tell the joke to the sentry. They are a clan by themselves, these soldiers of the line, and love nothing so much as a fight. Also they love no man more than the top cutter, the father of the company. The first sergeant is to them the leader of the clan and they acknowledge a greater loyalty to him than they do to the captain or the colonel. That was the reason why Beanie Bogan turned back—and why the sentry let him pass.

He waded across, chuckling, and, when he caught up with Whittle, he slapped him on the back.

"Whit, old boy," he declared with an oath, "you should have been a soldier. That's the soldier's way . . . never ask for help . . . just step into 'em with your own two hands. I knew by your eye you was thinking about that bastard . . . and, oh, Lordy, how I would love to've been there . . . but you never said a word, just tole me to go to hell and went out and cleaned him yourself. Oh, you had some help, did you? Well, I heard about that, too, but it was three to one, at the start, and Rico's *compadre* said you kept 'em all busy until they cracked you on the bean with a gun. Lemme feel of the place. *Aw*, that'll get well. Come on, let's go up to camp."

"I thought you quit Montaño," suggested Whittle, the better to change the subject. "You certainly talked that way."

"*Ahhr*, talk!" returned Bogan. "I always talk like that. It's the only way to get your pay. Look at them poor boobs in the Foreign Legion . . . two hundred a month and pickings . . . do you ever see 'em get their pay? Not a dollar, by grab. They're still bumming their tobacco and will, till we take Fronteras. But, say, do you think I'm going to lose out on the fireworks, after four-flushing around for months? *Ump-umm,* boy, there's loot enough in the Customs House alone to make every man jack of us rich. No, I'm going back to fight, and, if Montaño is afraid to, I'll hop in and take Fronteras myself!"

"You can't do it," challenged Whittle, but Bogan only grunted and kicked at a rock in the trail.

"Gimme a hundred trained soldiers," he answered deliberately, "and I'd take the town tomorrow. And I could go out to the fort and get that many deserters. Them boys is crazy to enlist, but I've got too much respect for the service. But these Mexicans will fight, if Montaño gives the word, and them Federals are just dying to quit. I've talked with their deserters . . . you remember that Yaqui Indian with the big three burned on his face? Well, he's a deserter, but they put their mark on him first. The major knew he was going to quit him, so he took the battalion branding iron and stamped a big three on his cheek. Well, Numero Tres says the men in his battalion had to be locked up in the *cuartel* every night and all their arms were locked up somewheres else, for fear they'd start a mutiny. A hundred fighting Irish could take the town."

"Well, why don't we take it, then?" asked Whittle impatiently, and Bogan clucked his tongue.

"When you get a Mexican to fight," he said, "you're pulling off a miracle. But they will fight, dad burn 'em, if you once get 'em started, but it's always *mañana! ¡Mañana!* They're out of ammunition, or they're short of guns, or they're waiting for somebody else, but the trouble with Pepe Montaño, as I found out today, is that the whole Montaño family has butted in. Up to a week ago, when he marched on Fronteras and the papers all took up this hooraw, they said he was crazy and everything else, but now they see a chance to win. It seems the southern Mexicans are starting a revolution, and Reyes is so busy right near home, he can't send up any more reinforcements. We isolated Chulita when we blowed up that bridge, and now here's Fronteras, ripe and waiting to be picked. And then the Montaño family butts in! What's their graft? Well, I'll tell you. They've formed a peace committee and they're talking over the wire with Reyes. Do you ketch the idee? If he'll come through with what they want, they'll call off little Pepe, who's always been the family goat, but, if Reyes won't, they'll tell Pepe to turn the bunch loose and Reyes will be left belly up. Because if we take that town with public sentiment what it is, it won't be two weeks until the United States will recognize Montaño as a belligerent. They'll have to recognize him, because he'll open up the Customs House and begin to do business anyway. And say, my boy, it won't be so bad to be a friend of Montaño's then. Look at the guns he'll be ordering, and the ammunition and equipment, and the artillery and machine-guns to boot. Oh, glory, and I know a man in town that would give ten thousand dollars to land the first contract for munitions.

"But listen here, Whit," he went on confidentially as they paused on the outskirts of the camp, "I've got a scheme, and I'll split with you half and half, but it calls for a little rough work. Now, sit down here a minute, where we won't be observed, and I'll tell you where you come in. It's all to our interest to pull off this battle in any way we can. Once we get it started, the Mexicans will join in, and then all hell wouldn't stop it. This Colonel Bracamonte that's in command of the town killed our wounded after the battle of Villa Nueva, and Pedro Espinoso and the rest of those bandits have sworn they'll have his blood. They've got him bottled up and they won't let him go, no matter what anybody says. But all the same, being Mexicans, they will sit around and wait. Now, here's the proposition. There's two things against us ... Montaño's family and this snaky Gambolier. That guy's a bad actor, you take it from me, and he's got to be put out of the way. You heard that crack I got off to Montaño about getting another military adviser? Well, that was just a starter. We've got to undermine him and turn the whole Foreign Legion against him. Now, I can't do that, because I enlisted some of them boys for a bonus of ten dollars a head, and the Irish never forget, but here's you, now, that enlisted when they did, and they'll listen to what you say. Just slip in among 'em and give this one some tobaccy and another a pleasant word, and then, when they take to you, just tell 'em about Gambolier and how he ditched us to save paying that ten thousand dollars. That'll settle the bastard because he's cold as a snake and they hate him like the devil already. But how to get rid of him. You're so kind of deceiving nobody would think for a minute that you'd fight, but someday in camp, when Gambolier comes through, you tax him with being a coward and with trying to get you killed. Then beat the face off of him, the way you did Pedley, and we'll laugh him out of camp. To get rid of him, that's the point, any way you can do it. Then we'll pull Montaño over the fence. We did it once, at the battle of Villa Nueva, but we got to got rid of this strategical Frenchman or we'll never smell powder again. As for the Montaño family, we'll just cut the wires on them and trust to luck for the rest. Now will you do that, Whit, me boy, or will I have to look further?"

"You'll have to look further," answered Whittle after a silence, "but I'll be there, when it comes to the battle."

"Ah, still thinking of the lady," observed Beanie sympathetically, "but, sure now, you're entirely wrong. You've no cause to be downcast. 'Twill all work out nicely, so put all them thoughts from your mind. You've come back a hero, with your name in the paper and your bold deeds on everybody's lips. 'The Dynamite Devil' they called you in the *Tribune*, and, sure, that's praise enough. They're all the same, I tell you, Whittle . . . those women all love a bold man, and then to have *him* come home with his face all disfigured from running against your fist! But there's one thing more you'll have to have to win the lady for sure and that's hard money in the bank. They're all the same there, too ... ye must have the money ... and how else can you get it but with me? So, come now, forget it, and, when I get to the loot, I'll lay aside a gift, like, for her."

"No, thank you, Beanie," answered Whittle from the darkness, "I'm afraid you don't understand. It's no use trying to help me ... the best thing I can do is to get killed."

"Ah, be a man!" reproached Beanie, and then, as his exhortations fell on barren ground, he muttered and went on to camp.

CHAPTER TEN

Beanie Bogan's plans for a benevolent mutiny, led and fathered by the turbulent Foreign Legion, were rudely disrupted and brought to naught by the arrival of Pedro Espinoso, a fire-eating, *gringo*-hating bandit who had left Montaño the week before. Of all the Mexican leaders he was the only man who refused to submit to delays. Prickly Pete, as he was called by the Americans, was the embodiment of brutal courage and he had wiped out the word *mañana* from his vocabulary. Having been a bandit for years, he was no dabbler in warfare, and, like the fighting Irish, he believed in direct action and results. But that was perhaps the only bond between them, for he hated the Foreign Legion as he did the *rurales* of Reyes.

He came riding into camp from one of his wild forays with 400 high-hatted outlaws at his back, and without mincing words he notified Montaño that he, Pedro Espinoso, intended to attack Fronteras immediately. With his men drawn up in military order and a mob of clamoring *insurrectos* behind him, he seemed for the moment to hold the high card and the Foreign Legion prudently withdrew. Then they argued and debated and bandied hot accusations, the bandits and Pepe Montaño, until at last Prickly Pete gained his point. Montaño agreed that Espinoso's cavalry should instantly surround the town while he, as soon as his artillery was available, would batter it down from the west. And meanwhile the army, which could no longer be restrained, was to engage the first line of entrenchments and drive the *pelónes* back to town.

So the bugles were sounded, the advance began precipitately, and, as the eager *insurrectos* in a disorderly mob went shooting and yelling into the fray, the Foreign Legion, eclipsed and forgotten, remained to bring up the artillery. This consisted of a single three-inch field piece, bored out of a seven-inch locomotive shaft and mounted on ponderous wheels. For months, in the machine shops of a captured mining camp, American mechanics under the direction of Gambolier had been laboring on this masterpiece, and now, as the Mexicans rushed forward to take the town, they dragged it slowly up the bluff. Gambolier, who had served in the French artillery, took charge of the emplacement of Long Tom, but before they had no more than got it on the mesa, the battle burst out below them.

From the brushy flats there came volleys and cheers as the *insurrectos* began their long-range attack, and then there was a *boom* from the *cuartel* at

Fronteras and a shell burst above the plain. As the flying shrapnel struck up a storm of dust, the attacking horde fell silent. The reckless firing of their .30-30s was checked as if by magic, and then *boom*, the gun spoke out again. *Bang*, crashed the shell as it burst far above them, and, as the scrap iron began to fall like rain in their midst, the insurgents broke for the hills. Gambolier had been right—with such undisciplined troops it was impossible even to menace the town. There were in Fronteras both field guns and mortars, and experienced gunners as well, whereas Montaño's men had never seen a cannon until they gazed upon the handmade Long Tom.

A superior smile came over Gambolier's face, as, with field glasses leveled at the plain, he watched the *insurrectos* retreat.

"Very well," he said, "if we are to be coerced by every bandit, let Espinoso take the town."

The panting Chihuahuans, their eyes big with terror, came crowding up to watch Long Tom's reply, but, although Montaño and his men both implored him to shoot it, Gambolier refused to serve the gun.

"No," he declared, "the attack was premature. Of what use is artillery now?"

"Ah, *tira le*," begged the Mexicans, making motions at the breech block, but Long Tom was not fired that day. The attack came to nothing, the Federals took heart, and Gambolier worked on placidly at his emplacement. As military adviser he had objected most strenuously when Espinoso had clamored for war, and now, jealous of his authority and determined to make the most of it, he resolutely refused to be hurried. And there were other considerations, known only to the Americans, that made it inadvisable to fire. It was a matter of doubt whether the breech block was safe—the question had been debated for days, and Beanie Bogan and other ex-soldiers insisted that it would blow up with the first shot. So for various reasons the Foreign Legion stood pat and let the Mexicans rage.

But if Gambolier, the military adviser, refused to take the attack seriously, there were others more hot-headed who had jeopardized their freedom in the belief that the great battle was on. That first, wild charge had proved too much for certain soldiers still wearing the United States uniform, and, when the fiasco was over, the despised Foreign Legion found itself recruited up to forty-five men. The new recruits had come across the river with their guns in their hands, ready to fight the whole Mexican nation, but when that day had passed, and the next, and the next, with no move to advance upon the town, the hearts of the deserters turned sick with disgust and then bitter with hate and scorn. Pedro Espinoso had subsided, contenting himself with tearing up the railroad track below Fronteras, but if Pedro in his anger had chastised Montaño with whips, the Foreign Legion chastised him with scorpions. Yet it all came to naught since Montaño and his peace committee were simply using their war ardor as a club to intimidate Reyes, and at last the word came that the dictator had capitulated and all was arranged but the terms.

Then the deluge broke and the outraged Foreign Legion demanded an immediate assault upon the town. As they gathered before the house where Montaño and his relatives were bartering away their last chance for a fight, it was Beanie Bogan, still the father of the company, who put their hot anger into words. At another time their invincible ardor would have won their commander's heart, but now Montaño begged them to be patient. A great victory, he said, was almost in their hands, and it could be gained without shedding blood, whereas, if they undertook to assault the town, many brave comrades at arms would be killed. So he begged their indulgence while he communicated still further with Reyes and Mexico City, and, if the surrender was agreed to, he would reward them even more than if they had taken Fronteras by force. So he spoke, but a high howl of Irish protest was the only response that he got.

The Foreign Legion as now suddenly constituted was composed almost entirely of ex-soldiers. Some there were who had bought out, and others had been honorably discharged, but a large number had deserted with their guns in the wild rush that preceded the battle. That was their business—to fight—and yet for three enlistments there had not been an echo of war. In the distant Philippines perhaps there had been a brush with the *ladrónes* or a clash with some naked hill tribes, but a real, open battle, such as young soldiers dream of, had not happened in all their world. And now, with all the makings of a battle before them, they were being balked by this man who talked peace!

Nor was their protest unseconded by the mountain Mexicans who had gathered for the assault of the town. There were many among them who were tainted with outlawry and proscribed by this same Porfilio Reyes. His *rurales* and soldiers had been pursuing them for years and, with the return of peace, would pursue them again. As the rumor spread of a possible understanding, of a peaceful surrender of all Mexico, they came in droves, led by their fiery chiefs, and registered a most violent protest. Once more Montaño, the dreamer and pacifier, appealed to their loyalty, but, just as he had them won over to be patient, Pedro Espinoso came dashing up. He rode a sorrel horse the color of burnished gold and brandished an angry pistol to clear his way, and, when he had confronted the chief of the *insurrectos,* he called him a coward and a traitor. It was not peace they wanted, but war—war against old Porfilio, war against Bracamonte and the Federals, who had murdered the Villa Nueva prisoners and shot all the wounded where they lay. What good would peace bring? It would simply give Reyes the opportunity to wipe them out. So raged Prickly Pete, the bandit chief of the Sierras, and all the lesser bandits swung their bats and yelled for war.

But Pepe Montaño, although he was not warlike, was fearless and he refused to be moved by their threats. He held out for peace and in the end they had a conference, which lasted two days and resulted in a Mexican proclamation. Montaño read it to his assembled army and won them over, to a man. In it he set forth that by the valor of his brave men he had struck fear to the heart of the dictator, but that now he must ask a final sacrifice of their devotion, greater even than the laying down of their lives. For the second time they had marched upon Fronteras and they now held it in their power, but, because it lay across the river from a friendly city whose inhabitants might be killed by flying shots, he was going to ask all true lovers of Mexico to withhold for a time their hands. The prize was theirs, but it must be spared and their valor turned to other exploits. Therefore, he had ordered an immediate advance upon the capital city of Chulita and in recognition of the services of the Foreign Legion, which had fought so bravely at Villa Nueva, he would give them the position of honor as leaders of the van.

Mere words, of course, and artfully devised to produce a certain effect, but, as the sun went down and the guns of Fronteras were shrouded in the protecting darkness, the Foreign Legion set forth. They marched out grumbling, for it was far to Chulita and a waterless desert lay between, but that word of tribute to Buck O'Donnell and the heroes of the vanished legion had won them in spite of themselves. Even Beanie Bogan, who knew Mexicans well, was disarmed by the reference to his friend. And Beanie, too, had received his mead of honor, for he also had fought at Villa Nueva. He bared his breast to show the new recruits the three furrows the machine-gun had plowed, and in the dramatic recital of that battle in the night he forgot the artful cunning of Gambolier.

Gambolier stayed behind, with his gun crew intact, to supervise the removal of Long Tom, but, as the legion marched off, with Bogan at its head, he mulled under cover of the darkness. A little hike, as he had suggested to Montaño, might divert the restless energy of the Americans, and, meanwhile, the peace committee could proceed with its negotiations without the continual menace of a mob. And if, for reasons of military necessity, it became advisable to reconsider their plan, a courier could be sent to recall the legion in ample time for the assault on Fronteras.

There was always something deep, something looking far ahead and providing against all possible contingencies, in everything that Gambolier suggested. This it was that won for the colonel the regard of Pepe Montaño, who was himself concerned only with dreams. He had conceived a great dream, of Mexico freed and ruled by justice alone, of its people dwelling in a communistic state wherein caste and class were abolished, but the necessary details of the bloody business that must precede such an ideal state, those must be conceived by others more apt. Having malice toward no man, how could he plot out the death of the poor *pelónes* who fought for Reyes? And, heartily despising the business of a soldier, how could he be interested in its inhuman strategy? No, he must leave that to Gambolier, and it was at Gambolier's suggestion that he ordered the advance upon Chulita.

The Foreign Legion marched out bravely, followed by the rag-tag of Montaño's army, which they soon left far behind. It was the pride of the infantrymen that they could outwalk a horse, and, now that the order to advance had been given, they swung off in route step down the road. Bo-

gan rode at their head, although not as their commander, for the new men were beyond all control,
and for an hour or more they hiked down the
road that led to the south and Chulita. In vain the
cowboys and civilian members called out from
the rear for a halt; the fever of long waiting was
like fire in their veins and the deserters pressed
on to the divide. There, with all Chihuahua before
them and Fronteras far behind, they sat down to
wait for the army and let the stragglers catch up.

They came in limping, and, as no army appeared, the footsore ones took off their boots. A
half an hour passed and the moon, which was
near its full, lit up the desolate desert like day.
One man after another stretched out in the road to
snatch a little sleep and still no army appeared.
Then Beanie Bogan rose up and, taking out his
field glasses, gazed long in the direction of the
town. It was almost midnight and their position
would be unenviable if they were caught out on
the desert at dawn.

"Well, what say, boys?" he ventured at last.
"Let's go back down the road and meet 'em."

"What, and walk clear back?" demanded Jimmy
Sullivan. "Let's go on until we come to a town."

"You'd find it a long walk," answered Beanie
soberly. "Come on, boys, they's been some mistake."

"What mistake?" asked Big Bill McCafferty,
rousing up from an uneasy sleep. "Have them
Mexicans took the wrong road?"

"No, that's just it," replied Bogan. "They's only
one road . . . and we're on it."

"Then they haven't started?" burst out Sullivan

angrily. "They just packed their horses for a bluff."

"I dunno," returned Bogan, "but I can tell you one thing . . . we're a long ways from water and grub."

"Well, damn a Mexican!" exclaimed Big Bill in a passion, rising up and grabbing his gun. "Let's go back and kill every last one of them . . . they've sent us with bags to ketch snipe!"

"You may be right, Bill," said Bogan, routing up the sleeping soldiers and starting them back down the road. "And if you are, this is no place for Martin Bogan's son."

CHAPTER ELEVEN

The advance upon Chulita, as Gambolier had surmised, had done much to abate the fighting fever of the legion, but the ignominious retreat, after having been tricked into starting, seemed to reverse that favorable process. As several hours of travel brought forth no signs of the following cavalry, or any of Montaño's advance guard, the footsore Americans extended their revilement to include the entire Mexican nation. Even the gallant general in whose name they invaded Mexico was not exempt from this universal execration, and, as daylight came on without revealing a sign of his army, Beanie Bogan added his voice to the chorus. Only one man remained silent and that was the Dynamite Devil.

Since he had crossed the river after his battle with Pedley, Bruce Whittle had lapsed into silence. He kept by himself and the wrangling of his companions fell unheeded upon his ears. He had a problem to solve and a decision to make, for it had become manifest at last that Constance's love for him was something more than a memory. She had followed him to Del Norte immediately after her marriage; she had sought him out in the plaza, and, although she had acknowledged Pedley's authority as her husband, she had not yielded to him in everything. For certainly, if he could command her absolutely, Pedley would have hurried his bride away, and the very fact that he himself remained argued the continued presence of Constance. The question was whether she had separated from her husband and, if so, what action Whittle should take.

Should he go back to Del Norte, braving officers and United States marshals and the certainty of landing in jail, for the poor consolation of one look into her eyes before he was denounced by her husband? Or should he, like a gentleman, stay quietly where he was and seek the ultimate solution in death? There were ways, of course, of sending her word but none of them escaped the objection that he was intruding where he had no right. Had he not bowed his head in voiceless shame when Pedley confronted him with his acts? It was true—he had gone to that lone house by the river in the hope of seeing Constance. And Constance was Pedley's wife. How much more then would he be humiliated if, after all that had happened, he persisted in his efforts to see her. And how could he again protest, if he were confronted by Pedley, that his motives were above reproach?

It was a long, bitter struggle, now with hope rising high, now with the certitude of defeat, until, in the end, he had ridden off with the Foreign Legion to accept whatever fate had in store for him. He would put it to the touch, this nice point of honor, and if, from the dangers and uncertainties before him, he escaped as he had before, then the hand of God, or whatever molds our destinies, would seem to be saving him—for her. But if, with all these other misfits, he should go out and be mowed down by guns, then the answer was plain and apparent to everyone and he would trouble his loved one no more. He would be dead, and for the dead there is nothing but tears, and a forgetting. It was better to pass on in silence.

He had gone out grimly, knowing the desert before him and the dangers that lurked for them all, but, as he turned back toward the line and saw death and dangers vanish, he was filled with an unutterable weariness. So it always came about—when he sought heroic death, it eluded him and left sordid hardship it its place. He got down from his horse and gave his place in the saddle to a runaway Texas boy named Jackson, whose high boots tortured his feet, and at daybreak, tired and hungry and out of water, he straggled with the rest past Fronteras. From the tracks in the dust it was now a certainty that Montaño's army had only started out and turned back, and, to add the last drop to their cup of bitterness, the Federal outposts opened up on them. They replied with a volley, then, as the artillery joined in, they turned and fled to camp.

They came straggling in, hot and sweaty from running and faint for something to eat, but the Mexican contingent had turned sullen and inhospitable and one camp after another refused them food.

"No tengo, hey?" snarled Big Bill McCafferty as

a black Chihuahuan showed his hands and said he had no food. "Then what you call this"—he hefted a flour sack—"and this?" And he picked up a strip of jerked beef.

"Not cooked," returned the Mexican, his eyes burning with resentment, and Bill grunted and went off with the beef.

But the poor camps of the *insurrectos* could not furnish food to the whole legion, even if the sulking peons had willed, and, led by Helge Wahlgren, they headed for the commissary while Bogan rode over to Montaño's quarters. There were certain things that he desired to know, and others that he wished to impart, but a hair-trigger atmosphere seemed to pervade the place and Montaño sent out word he was busy.

"Well, you tell him I'm *hungry!*" answered Bogan fretfully, but, fume as he would, he could get no audience until at last Gambolier appeared.

"General Montaño," he announced, "is engaged with very important business and must under no circumstances be disturbed."

"Oh," said Beanie, forgetting his hunger to give vent to an accumulation of spleen, "in connection with the advance on Chulita?"

"The advance," lied Gambolier, "has been abandoned for the present. And by the way, are those your men over there? Go and tell them to leave that commissary alone or I will report them to General Montaño!"

Bogan looked over his shoulder to where the Foreign Legion was surging up against the door of the commissary, and then he turned to Gambolier. "No," he replied, "those are your men, Mister Gambolier. And I thought General Montaño was busy."

A *crash* from the adobe that served as commissary was followed by a rush through the doorway, but, as the Americans swarmed in, the lazy Mexican camp became suddenly a seething ants' nest. From every campfire the envious *insurrectos*, who had been watching the legion from afar, leaped up and ran toward them, waving guns and brandishing pistols while the Americans stood on the defensive. As Beanie spurred over and tried to quell the riot, a fist fight broke out at the door and only the arrival of Espinoso's cavalry prevented a resort to arms. The Americans, starved and ugly, were in no mood to take dictation, and, even after Espinoso had dispersed the mob, they maintained their stand at the commissary. *Gringo* hater that he was, there was small hope indeed that Prickly Pete could arrest them without a battle and a war of words was bringing them rapidly toward that goal when Montaño himself appeared.

Under ordinary circumstances he was smiling and unruffled, but now by the look in his eyes as he shoved his way through the crowd it was evident that his patience was exhausted. They were blazing with anger, and, as the troops opened before him, he confronted the sullen legion.

"Come out of that house," he ordered tremulously. "Come out of it, every one of you!"

The Americans slunk out, some dropping their loot, others brazenly tucking food inside their shirts, and Montaño regarded them sternly.

"Sergeant Bo-gan," he commanded, turning to the shamefaced Beanie who had joined his renegade followers, "you will order your men to lay down their arms and march under guard to their quarters."

"They ain't my men," answered Beanie disrespectfully, "and I'll lay down my arms for no man. Colonel Gambolier is in command of the Foreign Legion, and you can give your orders to him." He hooked his thumb in the back of his belt and surveyed Espinoso and his bandits with scorn. "I've resigned," he declared, "and they ain't Mexicans enough in Mexico to make me give up my gun."

As Prickly Pete and his band of outlaws spoke only the language of the Sierras, the boldness of this statement escaped them, and Gambolier made haste to intervene.

"The Foreign Legion," he announced in formal tones, "is hereby disbanded and dishonorably discharged for willful insubordination. You will stack your arms and, within one hour, depart from the borders of Mexico."

A murmur of dismay and then of protest burst forth from the ranks of the deserters, and then Big Bill McCafferty stepped forth.

"I'd like to ask, sir," he said, coming to attention and saluting, "what act of insubordination you mean. I've a personal reason for not wishing to cross and I'm sure I've meant no disrespect."

Big Bill's personal reason was the moral certainty of being arrested and imprisoned as a deserter, but Gambolier had suffered too much in the past to be moved by pity now.

"It was the order of General Montaño," he answered stiffly, "that, pending the peace negotiations, no attack should be made upon Fronteras. But for the second time, upon your return to camp this morning, the members of the Foreign Legion have seen fit to disobey this command and for that reason you are dishonorably discharged."

"What, you'll bobtail us for fighting?" demanded McCafferty in a fury. "Well, to hell with an outfit like that! I can take these byes here and stand off the whole ahrrmy of you . . . and then to git a dis-honorable dis-charge!"

He picked up his gun and started for the river and the Mexicans prudently gave way, but in an instant he was back again, clamoring.

"I want me pay!" he demanded fiercely. "Four hundred and fifty dollars for the two months and more that I've served!"

"Yes, and me!" bellowed a great voice as Helge Wahlgren stepped forward with his little eyes glinting. "You pay me, or I don' know *what* I do!"

He wagged his huge head at every word and the crowd stood clamoring at his back. Beanie Bogan sat his horse and smiled.

"They'll never get it," he muttered to Whittle, and fixed his shrewd eyes on Gambolier. "*Ahr*, you rabbit-footed coward," he cursed under his breath, "you Mexicanized bastard, I know who framed this up. But God help poor Pepe if he lets you do the thinking for him . . . Prickly Pete will be chief in a week. Come on, Whit, we've got our ten thousand. What say if we skip across the bridge?"

"And get arrested?" inquired Whittle despondently.

"Well, let 'em arrest," responded Beanie. "I'll get you out of jail . . . come ahead."

"No, I . . . I'd rather not," replied Whittle, and Bogan looked him straight in the eyes.

"Say, lookee here," he said. "Be a man or a mouse. Don't let that greaser Pedley worry you. I'll run him out of town so quick and easy he won't know where's he at, and then you jump in and cop out the lady and get this thing off your chest."

"No, I've decided not to go back," answered Whittle firmly, and Beanie's argument was cut short by a yell from McCafferty that made the horses jump.

"Wan dollar!" he shouted, starting back from the doorway where Montaño stood surrounded by his guard. "Wan dollar! You owe me four hundred and fifty!"

"That is all I have now," answered Montaño firmly, "and you can take it or nothing at all. You have engaged in mutiny and refused to surrender your arms, and for that reason you have forfeited your pay."

"Nah ye don't!" threatened McCafferty, but, as he whipped up his gun, twenty rifles were leveled at his breast. There was a tense, anxious silence as Americans and Mexicans cocked their guns and stood waiting the attack, but no shot was fired, and, as Big Bill looked around him, he saw that the legion had lost.

"Well, gimme my money," he grumbled sulkily, "and to hell with you Mexicans, anyhow."

"Very well," replied Montaño, now quietly smiling, "you may march by and receive your pay. And in order to show I have no hard feeling against you, I will throw in a nice pair of socks."

"*Ahr*, yes, thankee," returned McCafferty with a gleam in his eye. "I wore out a pair last night."

CHAPTER TWELVE

Badly shaken by their misfortune, which would mean a penal term for some of them, the dishonorably discharged Foreign Legion took their dollars and filed dolefully down to the river. It was a mystery to them, still, how Montaño could dispense with them, the only trained fighting men he had—and obtained at such a cost in promises—and the shock had left them dumb.

At the edge of the stream Big Bill stopped.

What are you going to do, Bill?" asked Sullivan as McCafferty sat down on the bank, and Big Bill thrust out his lip.

"I'm going to try on me new socks," he said, "that I win at the battle of Fronteras."

"I'll go you one better." Sullivan grinned sociably. "I'm going to wash me feet."

"Sure, there's no hurry at all," responded Big Bill glumly. "It's Judge Duffy and the mill for us, the moment we cross the bridge. Why not take a swim, farther down the river, away from this crowd of rubbernecks, and maybe on the road we can think up some way to kape from being railroaded to Leavenworth."

"Let's go down to the dam," proposed Sullivan, jumping up, and soon, like a band of schoolboys, the whole legion was preparing for a swim. They went in by relays, for Pedro Espinoso was watching them with a jealous eye, and, when they had eaten a few oranges and apples that admiring Americans had thrown across the stream, they sat down to discuss ways and means. The situation was desperate for every one of them, for there were few indeed who could safely cross the river and their hour of grace was up. Already Prickly Pete had deployed his cavalry to prevent their return to camp and it was an open question whether he would not advance and force them to leave Mexican soil.

"Let's go down and join the Federals," suggested the impractical Sullivan, "and come back and clean out the bunch."

"Vell, I tell you vat I *vill* do," agreed Helge despondently, "I kill that feller Espinoso, if he comes."

"Yes, that's right," spoke up McCafferty. "We've took enough from him. I'm going to shoot him right through the hat. But look who's coming, with that American flag that we went off and left at the house. Yeh, old Beanie Bogan"—his voice rose insultingly—"that recruited us for ten dollars a head! They's no troubles for him . . . he's squared himself already while we poor divils must go to the mill."

"*Ahr*, you talk too much," retorted Beanie from

the distance. "Didn't I warn youse guys not to shoot at them outposts? Well, what's the use of crabbing at me when you brought it all on yourselves?"

He rode up before them, with Whittle close behind, and struck the shaft of the flag into the dirt.

"There's your flag," he said, "that those young ladies give you to place on the *cuartel* of Fronteras. But now, by Judas, you ain't got no flag nor country, and Montaño sends you this thing back." He motioned toward the flag that was a large American standard with a Mexican flag fastened across its center. "That's a hell of a flag," he went on bitterly, "neither one thing nor yet the other, and we might have made it famous. But no, you shanty Irish had to have the run of everything, and now you've got the straight kick. Montaño says to tell you to get across that river or he'll come down and put you across."

"Yes, he will," said McCafferty, laying hold of his rifle and jacking up a cartridge viciously.

"I tried to make a talk, boys," continued Bogan apologetically, "but Gambolier has got us in bad. He's told old Pepe that there'll never be any peace as long as there's an Irishman in camp, and I'm canned along with the rest."

"Serves you right," growled McCafferty. "What you going to do now? Can't you work it for us to join the Federals?"

"In the graveyard, yes," answered Beanie sarcastically. "Ain't we burned all their bridges twice?"

"Well, what *can* we do?" demanded Big Bill frankly. "I ain't a-going across until dark."

"So ye say," returned Bogan, "but look here who's coming like a bat out of hell. Get behind the bank, boys, and let me do the talking . . . it's nothing but Prickly Pete!"

He whirled his horse and swung in behind his men as Espinoso came dashing toward them. The bandit chief was mounted upon a shining golden sorrel that he had stolen from some ranch in his raids, and, as he reined in before them, a shower of gravel was thrown out by its plowing hoofs.

"Pigs of *gringos!*" he cursed in his low voice, and, swinging down from his saddle, he hurled their flag into the dirt. A torrent of threats and abusive epithets accompanied this astounding assault, and then Jimmy Sullivan leaped fearlessly out and caught the flag from the ground.

"You leave that alone, you dirty greaser!" he shrieked as he planted it on the bank, and for a moment they stood bristling, both yelling at once, like a pair of fighting dogs.

"Oh, you don't like it, hey?" barked Sullivan. "You don't like it even with this on it! Well, how will *that* do?" And with venomous swiftness he tore off the Mexican flag. "We're Americans," he cried, "and there's the old flag, and we'll fight for it until we die!"

He waved it in the air, and a rousing cheer rose up from the downcast Americans. A moment before they had been refugees and suppliants, desiring nothing more than to remain there on sufferance until they could slink across the river in the dark, but now in an instant they were caught up by the contagion and they cheered for the flag they had served.

"*¡Que caramba!*" shrilled Espinoso, drawing his pistol in a fury.

Then Bogan rode in on him with his gun. "Here. None of that," he said, jumping his horse against him, and, holding his six-shooter on him, he talked to him in Spanish. The wild, staring eyes of the bandit suddenly widened and he slavered at the mouth with rage, then, wheeling his horse, he thundered back to camp raising the war cry to summon his band.

"Into the river," yelled Bogan, grabbing Sullivan by arm and leg and hurling him into the stream, "and swim if you don't want to get shot!"

Sullivan came up sputtering, then, cooled by the water, he turned and struck out across the river. It was narrow at this point, just above the low dam, but hardly had he made a start, when, lashing his horse at the head of his troops, Espinoso came charging back.

"Get under the bank!" ordered Bogan quickly, and every man of the forty Americans dropped down and shoved out his gun. "Now hold your fire until I give the word." And Beanie stood erect behind them.

Espinoso came up like a thunderbolt, and, at sight of his menacing pistol, Sullivan dived and was lost to sight, but there were others interested besides the Mexicans and the legion—there were the American soldiers on the other side of the river. They had come out in force at the first sign of trouble, and now, as Jimmy Sullivan disappeared beneath the waves, they jerked up their rifles and challenged.

"Don't you shoot!" they warned in a chorus, and Espinoso lowered his gun. It was borne in upon him suddenly that, if he shot at the fugitive, the American soldiers would shoot at him—and even in his anger he was human. He knew that the Americans could shoot straight, and he knew also that he could not, and so he curbed his rage. Jimmy Sullivan came to the surface and ducked like a seal, and the next time he appeared he had floated to the dam and was under the guns of his friends.

"Aha, you dirty greaser!" he screamed back at Espinoso, and then turned and dodged behind the guard. But, foiled though he was by the escape of one recreant, Prickly Pete still saw a chance for revenge. The insulter of the Mexican eagle had fled from his just punishment, but the Foreign Legion was left. He turned to where they crouched beneath the Stars and Stripes and demanded in a tantrum that the flag be torn down, and, as the men of the legion defied him to touch it, his battle rage seemed to pass all bounds. Yet, here again, he was facing Americans, the picked fighting men of their kind, and it needed but a glance to convince the most confident that in a clash it would go hard with the Mexicans. They were out in the open, mounted upon prancing horses, and surrounded by a mad crowd from the camp, while the Americans were under cover with their guns at a rest and commanded by the iron-faced Bogan. So in the pinch his nerve cracked, and, when Montaño himself arrived, the American flag still waved above the soil of Mexico.

"What is the meaning of this disturbance?" he demanded impatiently after he had spurred his way through the throng. "Sergeant Bo-gan, you were ordered out of Mexico!"

"So I was," returned Bogan whose fighting blood was up, "but no low-browed Mexican *pelado* can come down and put me out."

He glanced hatefully at Espinoso as he spat out the word *"pelado"* and Prickly Pete responded with a rush.

"Ye-es, you're bad," taunted Bogan, when the rush had been stayed, "but you can get anything you want out of me!"

"What about this flag?" inquired Montaño more pacifically after he had listened to a tirade from Espinoso. "Don't you know you are on Mexican soil?"

"Yes, sure we are," admitted Beanie. "But after the deal we got from you, it's a cinch we're none of us Mexicans. We're American soldiers, and there's our flag, and you can go as far as you like."

There was another long and heated colloquy, in which Gambolier took the lead, and then Montaño spoke again.

"May I ask as a favor," he began quite pleasantly, "that you will take this American flag across the river?"

"Yes, sure you can," returned Beanie politely, "but will you kindly request Mister Espinoso to withdraw? I don't want that high-binder to get it into his nut that we give a damn for him."

Once more with great argument the conference was on and in the end Espinoso withdrew. With him went his cavalry, and, to save his face, he drove all the Mexicans before him.

"Now, Sergeant Bo-gan," said Montaño firmly, "I will ask you and your men to leave Mexico."

"All right, General Montaño," replied Beanie,

saluting, "we'll do that . . . when we get good and ready."

"Very well," answered Montaño, after gazing at him intently, and rode away to his camp.

"And now," burst out Beanie as soon as he was gone, "take this American flag across the river. It's been disgraced enough, God knows, by our cussedness, without being wallowed in the dirt by no Mexicans!"

He caught up the flag, which the combined forces of Montaño's army had not been able to cast down, and strode off with it down to the dam.

"Hey!" he called across to the seething mass of sightseers who had been watching the drama from afar, "is there a U.S. marshal over there? Well, tell him to go to hell and send out your ranking non-com to take charge of the national colors!"

There was a rumble of laughter at this soldier's jest, and the sergeant of the guard, after taking off his shoes, waded out and received the colors in mid-stream. The great crowd of Americans, roused to a frenzy of patriotism by the gallant defense of the flag, gave way to cheer after cheer, but, as Bogan and his men were staging a salute to the colors, there was a volley from the Federal trenches in front of Fronteras. *Rrrr-rap* went the guns, like tearing a blanket, and then bullets began to splash into the river.

"Now what?" exclaimed Bogan, and, glancing swiftly down the stream, he saw a lone man on the Mexican skyline. It was his partner, Bruce Whittle, standing erect like a soldier and firing back at the Federals. And, running swiftly toward him, tottering in his tight boots, was the sore-footed Texas boy, Jackson.

"Here! Come back here!" yelled Bogan as his soldiers started off on the run, then, plunging back to the shore, he grabbed up his gun and went splashing through the water after them.

CHAPTER THIRTEEN

When the faint-hearted Mexicans retired from their charge and left the Foreign Legion un-harmed, the last of Whittle's illusions were swept away and he saw the "war" as it was. The terrifying machine of death to which he had committed himself in the hope of a speedy release was no more than a tinsel plaything, a mockery of actual war. Its generals were palterers, its soldiers were cowards, its battles mere wars of words. They rushed at each other like angry dogs, bristling and snarling and showing their teeth, and then, after each ignoble encounter, they drew off grimly and growled. But of fighting there was none—no charges, no assaults, no attacks upon the town, only quarrels and bickerings and wasted days. And in the end Whittle picked up his gun and started off down the river.

Behind him he heard the boasts of the desert-ers as they bawled across to the crowd of Ameri-

cans, and with a sense of escaping from a bedlam
he hurried away by himself. What to him were
the petty machinations of Gambolier, the futile
negotiations of Montaño, the foolish rantings
about liberty and equality? No more than the
flannel-mouthed bombast of the legion, always
talking of its rage for battle but as carefully
avoiding a fight. They were words, mere words,
when what was needed was a blow, even if struck
by a single man. He mounted the bank, far down
the river, and looked across the plain at the town.

The Federal colonel in command at Fronteras
had been educated at the Military College of Cha-
pultepec, and, while Montaño and his advisers
had been busily doing nothing, he had been as
busily digging trenches. Fully a mile from the
plaza of the straggling town he had thrown up
his first line of defense, and behind that another,
showing dimly in the distance, in which to keep
his reserves. Yet between Whittle and these
trenches there was a natural defense far superior
to either of the Federals', the banks of the canal
that flowed, wide and deep, through the outskirts
of the town. And besides there was the riverbank,
some ten feet high in places, extending halfway
down to the bridge. Behind its shelter a man
could creep far down the stream, and then rise up
and rake the trenches if only he had the nerve.

Whittle stepped into the water and waded
down farther, and then climbed up on the bank.
What small respect he had once had for Mexican
marksmanship had been dispelled by the attack
of the morning, for of all the 1,000 bullets that had
been fired at the legion not one had found its

mark. So he did not flinch when an outpost saw him and sent a bullet over his head. Another followed, and then another, so near that it made him jump. He saw the man, crouching behind a mesquite tree not far from the first-line trench, and sent a bullet back. Although much of his later life had been spent in the workshop, he had learned when a boy to shoot with the best of them and his shot struck close to its mark.

There was a lull as the Federals rose up in their trenches to see from whence the shot had come— and then there came that first volley of bullets that had diverted Bogan from his salute to the flag. The bullets going past sounded like a flight of swift-winged blackbirds, so wildly did the Federals shoot, and Whittle laughed for the first time in ten days. Life had been a drab affair, dragging about with Beanie Bogan or listening to the loud-mouthed legion, but this woke the fighting spirit in his breast. They were children, these Federals, little scared Indian children, playing with weapons that had been made for better men, and yet Montaño and his army and the boastful Foreign Legion had been afraid to make an attack. They had hidden in the foothills, half-starved and out of everything, for fear of men like these. He raised his rifle in a mocking gesture and fired back at the Federal army.

Then they came in good earnest, but a mile too high, the whispering Mauser bullets that, if one should happen to hit him, would pass through his vitals and on. He dropped down behind the bank, shooting back defiantly, and, as he paused to refill his magazine, he heard a man running up behind him. It was Tight Boots, the boy upon whom he had taken pity in their long hike back to camp, and behind him came others of the legion, all running.

"Stay with 'em!" yelled Tight Boots, plumping down behind the bank and shoving out his .30-30. "Stay with 'em, Dynamite. Stick till hell's no mo'!"

He cut loose at the trenches, and, as the others came up, they answered with volley for volley. Beanie Bogan came up, panting and cursing recklessly, and soon the full-mouthed *bark* of his .30-40 Special was added to the *pop* of .30-30s. The roar from the trenches rose to battle height as the Federals replied to their volleys, but the blood lust of his ancestors had been roused in Bruce Whittle and he jumped up and started down the river.

"Where you going?" cried Tight Boots, and, not receiving any answer, he scrambled up and followed after him. "Come on!" he yelled back. "Who's afraid of them Mexicans? We're going to take the town!"

The legion looked after them, then, one after the other, they went splashing on down the stream. It was not much of a river, over half of its water being diverted to fill the enormous canals, and, as Whittle led the way down its wide sandy bed, he found himself the leader of the charge. So in ancient days the patriot Robert Bruce, whose blood still ran in his veins, had charged against the enemy, and after his death his stout heart, hurled before them into the thick of the battle, still led men on.

"Heart of Bruce, lead us on!" the Scotch warriors had cried, and, as his heart, encased in a casket, fell to the earth in the midst of the foes, they

charged in and won it back. It was the blood now
that spoke and Whittle, the jeweler, the man who
had lost his lady love by indecision and doubt,
charged in to win victory or death. He was the
leader now and bold Beanie Bogan found himself
bringing up the rear.

"Hey! Wait!" he called as Whittle climbed up
the bank where he could rake the Federal trench
from end to end. "Don't shoot, boys!" he implored. "Let's make it a volley and clean 'em before they can shoot back!"

"Well, all right," agreed Whittle, "you can take
charge of it now . . . I just came down here to start
something."

"Ah, nah, nah!" exclaimed Bogan slapping him
jovially on the back. "You pull this off yourself.
What's the big idee . . . going to take the town? All
right, I'll be your military adviser."

He climbed up the bank where the excited soldiers were peering over at the enemy and jerked
them swiftly back.

"Keep your heads down!" he commanded.
"Don't show 'em a hair until we rise up and give
'em a volley. Break the bank down first and dig in
on the edge, and every man build up a good rest."
He hurried down the line, placing each new man
as he arrived, and at last, as he went past Whittle,
he touched him and pointed up the river. "You've
started something, all right," he said, and laughed
to himself as be went on. Whittle looked up the
river and saw a swarm of *insurrectos* pouring
down toward the position the legion had held,
and up on the mesa overlooking the plain the big

hats were bobbing everywhere. "This'll drive Pepe crazy"—Bogan grinned as he came back—"but what do we give a damn!"

He looked over the bank at the long line of Federals, lying unconscious of their danger in the trench, and slapped the butt of his gun.

"By grab"—he chuckled—"I wouldn't miss this for a hundred thousand dollars . . . keep your heads down! Do you want to draw their fire? Now, stop and get your breath, and, when I give the word, push your guns out and aim down that trench. You've been shooting worse than Mexicans . . . now I want you to shoot careful. Set your sights at four hundred and remember what that hindsight is for. You can aim now . . . hold 'er steady, and pick out your man. Now . . . ready, fire!"

The volley ripped out, and, as the dust arose along the trenches, Beanie Bogan gave a wild yelp of joy.

"They're cleaned," he cried, "like a ditch full of rabbits! We've got 'em going, boys! Give 'em hell!"

He raised his gun, which he had held regretfully, and added his shot to the rest, and then the startled Federals broke and ran. In an instant, where before the space had been vacant, it was alive with flying men. They ran helter-skelter, throwing away their guns and bandoleers, and the legion let out a yell. It was answered from up the river, and then from farther up, and then there came a supporting volley from the mesa, which was dotted with Montaño's men.

"Cease firing!" commanded Bogan, passing swiftly down the line. "Cease firing, you danged idiots! Do you want to draw some shrapnel? Well, key down then, and let the *insurrectos* go in!"

A high Mexican yell, gaining volume every moment and punctuated by the rattle of arms, rose up from the mesa and plain, and then, while the legion looked on in wonder, the Montañistas charged. From wherever they were, whether under the riverbank or massed along the edge of the mesa, they poured out across the brushy plain and ran on toward the deserted line of trenches.

"The poor, ignorant bastards!" exclaimed Beanie half pityingly. "They think they done that themselves! Well, holy jumping Jehut, will you look at them charge now? But oh my, when them Federal field guns get their range!"

There was a long minute of waiting while the unorganized *insurrectos* rushed forward to drop into the first trenches, and then with a *crash* a shell burst above them and struck up a long line of dust. *Boom!* spoke out the cannon from the *cuartel* in Fronteras, and then another, and another broke loose. There was a puff of white smoke in the clear, upper air, a slash of flying shrapnel, and still another report, and for the second time the *insurrectos* turned, and fled. They were peons from the mountains, unused to plains and cities and the terrifying cannon of the Federals, and they ran, although more from terror than from fear.

But, despite the disorderly milling to and fro of his men, there was still discipline in Montaño's camp and scarcely had the baffled *insurrectos* sought shelter along the riverbank when the provost guard fell upon them. Down the river they came, a double column of men commanded by dancing officers, and, as they rounded up their soldiers and drove them back to camp, a single officer left the rest behind and pursued the recalcitrant legion.

"Let 'im come," said Bogan, looking back up the river, "it's only Gambolier. But what shall we say, boys, when he orders us back . . . shall we quit now or go take the town?"

"Take the town!" they yelled in a chorus of cheers, and Beanie regarded them with a fatherly smile.

"Well said, me brave byes," he observed, relapsing into Irish. "And, the way I feel now, with me belly shrunk to nahthing, I would fight the whole bloody garrison for one dish of tortillas and beans."

He plunged into the water and, despite the shouts of Gambolier, led the famished legion down the stream. But though he gave the orders, as father of the company and by virtue of his service as sergeant, he accorded to Bruce Whittle the place of honor as leader of the advance. Their position now was desperate, with the Federals before them and the hostile *insurrectos* in the rear, but the wine of victory had given them new strength and they were marching hopefully toward the tortillas and beans. As to just how a company of forty-four men could take Fronteras in time for supper the rank and file was a bit hazy, but Beanie Bogan had led many a forlorn hope, and they followed him with absolute confidence. And bravest of the brave, for he felt no fear of death, was the man with the heart's blood of Bruce. They called him Dynamite, after the bridges he had wrecked, and at last he felt that his hour was coming. Here was the desperate attack, the heroic assault that he had dreamed of and desired for a month, and he led on like the Bruce of old.

At a point down the river where a goat trail climbed the bank the legion crept up and looked across at the town. *Pow!* went a Mauser, and, as the Federals saw their enemies so close upon them, they opened up a veritable fusillade. But the men of the legion were trained to close shooting as well as to keeping cover and more than one white-capped soldier, rising up to find his target, was struck down by their well-aimed bullets. Yet hardly had this second long-range skirmish begun when Gambolier came panting up from behind. He was white with rage, for Montaño's peace negotiations—which were at that moment being carried on over a special wire direct to Mexico City—had been brought to a standstill by this precipitate attack, and, if it kept on—if those scapegraces persisted—the last hope of peace was lost.

"Cease firing!" shouted Gambolier, whipping out his sword and rushing up to the men. "Cease firing immediately! By order of General Montaño!"

"Who's he?" inquired McCafferty, looking up from his sniping, and then he saddled his face against the stock.

Bang! spoke out his Springfield, and, as he worked the bolt, Big Bill stuck his tongue in his cheek. "Niver mind!" he observed, while the rest turned to listen. "Sure, we mean no disrespect at all! But our backs is bruck with packing these heavy cartridges and we're shooting the brutes away!"

"Sergeant Bogan," appealed Gambolier, turning to the grinning Bogan who was directing the fire from behind, "please order your men to stop. General Montaño is in the midst of some very delicate negotiations which may lead to far-reaching results, but if the Federal commander should report this attack, it might destroy our last prospect of peace."

"I'm a soldier," answered Bogan. "What do I care about peace? We're going in to take the town!"

"Ah, but listen," cried Gambolier in an agony of impatience, "you must . . . you must make them stop! Name your price . . . any reward . . . but positively . . . absolutely . . . this firing must instantly cease!"

"I haven't got any price," returned Beanie sourly, and hunched up against the bank. The moment had come that he hardly dared hope for, when he would have the tricky Gambolier in his power, and now he was enjoying it to the utmost. Along the edge of the broken-down bank the roistering members of the legion were laughing and shouting as they shot. No one had been injured, there was nothing to detract, and Gambolier only added to their joy. Even the silent Whittle, who had before seemed so quiet, was a leader in the fighting. Gambolier looked them over, to find a single one he could appeal to, and then he turned back to Bogan.

"Sergeant Bogan," he warned, "I will hold you personally responsible if you do not stop this firing at once."

"But I told 'em to stop," complained Beanie, grinning maliciously, "and they told me to go to blazes. Why don't you stop 'em yourself?"

"I will!" exclaimed Gambolier with military decision, and, drawing his sword, he slapped the nearest man on the rump. "Cease firing!" he commanded, passing swiftly down the line, "cease firing, sir! And you! And you!"

There was stunned and startled silence, then Big Bill got up and grabbed their ex-commander from behind. "Hey," he said, jerking him down behind the bank and wresting away the castigating sword, "who called you in on this? Now you beat it . . . understand? And tell Pepe Montaño we're trying to earn that dollar!"

He gave him a start and threw his side arm after him, but Gambolier whirled about before he fled to hurl back a parting threat.

"You'll pay for this!" he burst out spitefully. "I've warned you, and that's enough. Now, if you don't cease firing, I will call out our troops and have you shot down from behind!"

He raced off up the river, thin and spidery in his riding boots, and the grin left Bogan's face.

CHAPTER FOURTEEN

The sinister figure of Colonel Gambolier had hardly disappeared up the river when the vigilant Beanie Bogan, who had been watching his flight, called Whittle from where he was firing.

"There they come," he said, pointing at a line of high hats that was rapidly advancing toward them. "Now what are you going to do?"

"Who are they?" asked Whittle. "They may be our friends. I certainly wouldn't fire on them."

"Don't you think they're our friends," returned Bogan. "This is regular Mexican stuff. They're coning down here to arrest us. Yes, look at that bastard in front, holding up his hand for peace . . . they never can play the game straight."

He glared at them a minute, then, as they came within earshot, he shouted at them fiercely to stop.

"¡No tira!" shrilled the Mexicans, still making the peace sign, and once more they came hurrying on.

"Go on back there!" yelled Beanie, leaping out into the open and waving them back with his gun, but the Mexicans were hard to stop.

"¡No! ¡No tira!" they called as the legion ceased firing and lined up to repel an attack. "¡Amigos! ¡Muy amigos!"

"Amigos, nothing!" cursed Bogan. "It's a guard of them high hats that Gambolier's sent down to arrest us. Well, come on. Whit, you're running the bunch . . . shall we shoot 'em up or not?"

"No, let 'em come," answered Whittle with sudden decision. "They can't arrest us anyway."

"¡Vaya se!" roared Beanie. "Get back there, you damned greasers! I'm going to drop a bullet in front of them!"

"I'll tell you," cried Whittle, "let's go on down the river and dare 'em to come and get us. That's a fair test, boys, and, while we're about it, we'll rake that second line of trenches!"

He splashed off down the stream, and once more the legion tagged on in spite of itself. Whittle was nothing to them; he was not even a trained soldier, but when he led off, they could not help but follow, and Bogan came on grumbling behind. He was an old campaigner and he knew all too well that bravery alone counts for nothing; yet with his partner in the lead he dared not interfere, for Whittle had rebuked them all by his courage. So he lingered in the rear, menacing the Mexicans with his rifle, until at last they fell behind. The legion turned a point and plunged into a willow thicket, and, when they came out on the other side, they could see the international bridge below them.

"Ah, here now!" burst out Bogan as they were

about to advance. "This is grand, boys, this is no-ble, but by the Pope's toe you can't charge right in and take that town. It's all right, under this bank, but when we step out into the open, them machine-guns will mow us down. We've got to have leadership and military dis-cip-line, or we'll go out like the other boys at Villa Nueva."

"That's right," agreed Whittle, turning back from the lead. "You go ahead, Beanie, and we'll do whatever you say."

"Oh, nah, nah!" protested Bogan as the legion ac-claimed him. "It ain't that I want to lead . . . but I saw 'em all killed in less than a minute, and I got these three wounds here myself." He pointed to his breast where the machine-gun had creased him and blinked as the legion stood silent. "We're in a hell of a fix, boys," he went on earnestly as the soldiers gathered about him, "and I'd hate to see you wiped out like that. But if you'll follow my orders . . . what I learned then and since . . . I believe we can take the town. But think it over and remember this . . . if you start out with me on this flyer, I don't want any man to turn back. They's some of you here in the U.S. uniform, deserters from the United States Army, and I'd take shame to think that any American sol-dier had ran away from a Mex. So think it over, and all in favor will hold up your hand good and high."

The hands shot up, for the legion was with him, and Bogan's eyes gleamed with pride.

"Well and good," he said, "and, if you follow my orders, we'll make Mexican the court lan-guage of hell."

Sending back a rear guard to observe the *insur-rectos* and dividing his men into rough squads,

Sergeant Bogan beckoned Whittle, and they crept off together to view the approaches to the town. The high bank of the river, which had given them shelter, here flattened to a low, mud slope, but across a field of corn there rose the bank of the canal, piled high with silt, leading down between the river and the town. And on the farther side, striking the arc of a circle just outside the first scattered huts, was the Federals' second line of entrenchments.

"It's a cinch," declared Bogan, turning hastily back, "but what the divil is that?"

A few scattering shots from up the river merged suddenly into a fusillade, and, as they crouched down in the willows, the Federals in the second line of trenches opened up with a smashing volley. Then the rear guard came running, their faces all a-grin, and Beanie called his men to arms.

"Ah, that's it," he said as the guard reported, "fellers was a bunch of fighting *insurrectos* that had broke loose and gone to it like us. And bet a dollar," he burst out suddenly, "that they're led by Numero Tres. That was him up in front, the dad-burned Indian, trying to flag us by making the peace sign! Well, in we go, boys. This is pretty lucky, for everybody except them Federals. We'll slip across the cornfield to the canal and rake their trenches, while they're busy with Number Three, and after that . . . oh, Judas, come on, we got to get in on this."

A steady roll of rifle fire was coming from the trenches, and, as they went wriggling like snakes through the corn rows, leaving a wake of waving tops where they passed, the soldiers at the guardhouse that defended the bridge head opened up on the *insurrectos*. Yet, hardly were they installed against the bank of the ditch, when the Federals at the bridge made them out, and the flight of bullets that had been going over their heads came slashing into the dirt.

"Into the ditch!" commanded Bogan as the men began to flinch, and, springing up from cover, he leaped recklessly over the bank. The legion went after him, their breath held for swimming, but the wide-flowing canal had gone dry. It seemed a miracle at the time—although some wily *insurrecto* had merely turned off the water at the head gate— but the soldiers did not stop to wonder. They scrambled down the bank and up the other side and, thrusting out their guns, drew down on the line of shooting Federals. The trench began not far from them, on the edge of the town, and swung in a slight curve across the plain, and within it they saw the soldiers in their white caps and uniforms huddled down like rabbits in a hutch.

"Pick your man!" called out Bogan as they leveled their guns, and, when their volley ripped out, every soldier in the trench leaped up. Some were hit, some scared, some still flighty from the panic that had driven them from the first line of entrenchments, but as the volley of bullets raked the length of their shelter every man sprang up and fled. It was a rout, a stampede, a wild rush for safety, and the legion emptied its guns into the mass.

"Cease firing!" ordered Bogan as the last frightened Federals fled before the lash of their bullets.

"Cease firing and follow me down the ditch!" But not a man stirred, the blood lust had taken hold of them and they lingered for shot after shot.

"Fall in!" he yelled as a sudden splash of bullets threw the dust up in their faces and then, as a bullet came down the ditch, he swung his rifle and struck the flats of their feet. That fetched them up standing, but, as he started down the canal bed, running free on the firm, wet sand, a fusillade of shots broke out before them, and the bullets came bouncing up the ditch. One man went down, his foot struck out from under him by the smash of a ricochet shot, and then at a volley Bogan leaped up the bank and fell flat on the other side. The legion followed, burrowing down into the sand and rank weeds, where fresh bullets seemed to search them out. Like angry hornets whose nest has been stoned, the Federals came swarming down the causeway from the town, and an outburst of firing from the guardhouse by the bridge made one side of the canal bank as bad as the other. Bogan thrust out his gun and began firing down the ditch, where the Federals had raked them from a bridge, but the battle was unequal and the legion was giving ground when Bruce Whittle leaped up from his place.

Across the flat, between them and the guardhouse, there stood a long, low adobe house, a fortress in itself, and, while the legion looked doubtfully after him, he made a run for it. The time had come for which he had longed, when he could put his courage to the test, and, as the bullets zipped by him or tore up the ground, he charged straight into the storm of gunfire.

For the moment he was a target of every Federal who had a cartridge in his gun, but a great strength, an elation bore him on through the hail until his feet seemed barely to touch the ground. He was flying through the air, spurning the earth beneath him, and the goal was not far ahead.

The door of the house, painted a violent Mexican blue, stood out against the gray walls like the entrance to a haven of refuge. A bullet smashed into the door frame and little puffs of dirt were struck out from the mud of the wall, and then he sprang against the door. It gave, but only the length of a doubled chain that was padlocked about the frame, and, as he fell back baffled, a glancing bullet struck his rifle and knocked it from his hand. He rose up dazed, and then a man dashed by him and shook the door to its moorings. Another and another, as fast as they came, went smashing against the frame until at last Helge Wahlgren, the terrible Dane, came hurtling like a battering ram and fell, door and all, inside the house. In a wild rush they went over him, and, when the scramble was past, twenty men were safely inside. The rest were gone, lost somewhere in the storm of bullets that was beating outside their fort, searching out every crevice to get to them.

CHAPTER FIFTEEN

While the Foreign Legion, against orders, against reason, and all the known rules of military strategy, was fighting its way down the river in quest of tortillas and beans, another anomaly, quite as rare in military circles, was being enacted before Montaño's camp. General Montaño, who had marched with his Army of Liberation to batter down the gates of Fronteras, was taking the guns from the hands of his soldiers and sending them to camp under guard. The *insurrecto* attack, so impotent and ill-advised, and so barren of any results, was cut short by the command of their chief, and, as they withdrew, disgruntled and protesting, the Americans were left to their fate. They had disobeyed their orders and been discharged from the army and their valor could not plead for them now.

Within the mud walls of the lone adobe house Beanie Bogan found less than twenty men. The rest had fallen out in the rush down the ditch and now they were lost to the legion. Where they were, no one knew, nor could they stop to inquire, for their shelter had become a target for many guns. From the guardhouse by the bridge the bullets came in volleys, *thudding* spitefully against the thick walls, and from a barricade up the main street the spitting muzzle of a machine-gun added its torrent of flying lead. Yet no shots spat back in answer, for Bogan was counting his cartridges while his sharpshooters dug loopholes through the walls.

"Let 'em shoot," he said, "and, when they've had their fling, we'll show 'em a little marksmanship. We're short, boys," he announced, "ain't got thirty rounds apiece . . . and, when that's gone, we're done for. So you that can't shoot give to them that can and save ten apiece for a rush."

He passed about the walls of the darkened room, doling out the spare cartridges to his best marksmen, and then he took his post by a loophole. It commanded the street from which the machine-gun belched, and he aimed long before he ventured a shot.

"Wan," he crooned, relapsing into Irish, "I beaned him, the son-of-a-bitch." He waited patiently while his men lay and watched him, and then once more he shot. "Two," he counted. "Take your time to it, Helge. We've put that machine-gun on the bum."

"Then vy not make a run for it?" demanded Helge from his loophole. "Dey ain't nothing to eat in dis house!"

"Wait till night comes," returned Beanie sooth-

ingly, "and, if the other boys don't come, we'll try
to make a gitaway across the river."

"Yes, and get sent to Leavenworth," answered
Helge, the deserter, but Bogan only grunted.

Outside the house, where the noonday sun beat
down, the bullets still *thudded* and *pinged*, but, as
he made his rounds, peering out through each
loophole, Bogan let out a yell of joy.

"Here come the boys!" he cried. "Big Bill and all
the rest of them! And there's some Mexicans tag-
ging along behind . . . it must be Numero Tres and
his bunch!"

A mad outburst of firing from the bank of the
river announced the *insurrecto* approach, and,
well to the front but crouching low, Beanie could
see McCafferty and his soldiers and the irrepress-
ible Tight Boots. Farther back up the river, the
high hats of the insurgents bobbed and ducked as
they advanced down the stream, and from across
the Río Grande, where the Americans looked on,
he could hear a high Texas cheer.

"Here we are, Bill!" he yelled, waving a rag out
the window, and then, grabbing up his gun, he
made a dash for the door. "Ah, come on!" he
cried. "Let's go out and at 'em! The bastards are
beginning to run!"

He plunged through the doorway, his face all
a-grin, but Helge was out before him. Behind him
came the rest, scarcely heeding the bullets, rushing headlong for the guardhouse by the bridge.
From far up in town a machine-gun broke loose,
spraying the flat with a torrent of lead, but the legion seemed to hold a charmed life. A few scattered shots spat out from the guardhouse as they

began their unpremeditated assault, but when they gained the entrance, the garrison was in full flight, leaving behind their guns and their dead.

At last the reckless Americans, starved and harried and driven about, had a shelter from the wrath of their enemies, and a source of food and supplies. While outside the brick guardhouse the bullets lashed the treetops and went skittering along the causeway to the bridge, Helge Wahlgren charged the kitchen where the Federals had abandoned their dinner, and Bogan searched the quarters for cartridges. Then Big Bill McCafferty and his band of men came storming in under cover of the causeway, and from across the river where the Americans were watching there came a mighty cheer.

It was sweet to their ears after their battling and outlawry, and, even though Big Bill had left two of his men sorely wounded in his hurried retreat, the legion gave an answering yell. Then with eating and drinking and caring for the wounded, the hours were quickly sped, and, as evening came on, Numero Tres crept in grimly, followed by a remnant of his fighting men. They had been hiding in the willows, sniping across at the Federals who lay behind barricades of sandbags on the flat-roofed houses of the town, but a machine-gun on the cathedral had searched out their shelter and driven most of them up the river in retreat. Yet Number Three was satisfied—he had escaped Montaño's provost guard and the night would bring fighting for them all. Bogan greeted him cordially, for there was work for all of them if the town was to be stormed that night, and the hungry *insurrectos* were led to the kitchen while he perfected his plans for the attack.

The Federal fire had ceased abruptly—upon notice from the American commander at the bridge that bullets were coming into Del Norte—and, as night came on, an ominous silence settled down over battle-scarred Fronteras. On the American side the vast crowds of people, who had resisted all efforts to force them back, now dispersed on account of darkness, and, as the danger seemed past, the officer of the guard allowed a single man to go across the line. All day, while the machine-guns had raked the bridge and the Mausers had spattered the town, the iron-faced regulars had stood at their post and turned back every man who applied, but when Gambolier, as a messenger of peace, appeared and stated his case, the officer of the guard passed him on with a heartfelt sigh of relief. Hence Beanie Bogan's surprise when, as he was marshalling his men, Gambolier stepped in upon them.

He was stern, yet not too stern, and in the depths of his eyes there was a flicker of light that betokened uncertainty and fear. He faced once more the fighting Foreign Legion, which had been dismissed by Montaño in disgrace and yet, single-handed, had raked two lines of trenches and driven the Federals before them. It had been a great victory—but not for Montaño. Instead, his prestige and that of his army had suffered a terrible blow, and his negotiations with President Reyes, in spite of his best efforts, had been brought to the verge of failure. But one thing could save them—to recall this fighting legion and nip the impending battle in the bud.

"Gentlemen," began Gambolier as they gazed

at him in astonishment, "I bring a message from General Montaño."

"Damn," cried Big Bill, motioning him away with his gun, "we got no use for him nor you!"

"Well, what is it?" demanded Bogan, cutting short the impending wrangle. "Shut up, Bill, and let him spit it out."

"General Montaño wishes me to notify you," announced Gambolier solemnly, "that you have committed an invasion of Mexico, the penalty of which is death."

"Aw, cripes!" burst out Bill, but Bogan met his eye and he relapsed into mutinous mutterings.

"But," went on Gambolier with a reassuring smile, "he has given his word . . . if you will desist from this attack and return forthwith to camp . . . to pay you in full for all your back time and take you back into his service. Otherwise, you are filibusters in the worst sense of the word and subject to instant execution."

"How do you figure that out?" inquired Bogan after the hotheads had had their say.

"In this way," returned Gambolier as they hushed their clamor to listen, "you are no longer in Montaño's service. You were formally discharged at the river this morning and warned to depart from Mexico. But instead you began an attack upon this city, which he had forbidden under pain of death, and, in returning your fire, Federal bullets have crossed the boundary and killed half a score of Americans. For that reason you have been outlawed by the United States government and the President has given orders that you shall be dealt with the greatest severity, and General

Montaño has given formal notice that he will grant you no quarter when caught. But in spite of all this, because of the past services of the Foreign Legion, General Montaño still offers you his complete forgiveness, if you will immediately surrender to me."

"And if we don't?" challenged Bogan as his men fell to muttering. "What will General Montaño do then?"

"He will order his men," answered Gambolier impressively, "to close in and take you from behind. And to make your punishment more certain he will declare a truce with the Federals until the last man has been captured or killed."

"Oh," said Bogan, and by the dim light of captured candles he gazed at the faces of his men. For a day and a night they had been marching and fighting and suffering endless hardships and yet they were still set and grim. They would not yield easily and, coming from Gambolier, the threat had been received with bad grace. He it was who had framed up the false start to Chulita, in order to get them out of the way, and now, once more, he stood before them with a threat of instant death. Yet, if Montaño made good his threat—if under cover of night, he sent his troops down the river to cut off their escape from the town—they would be left in desperate straits. And Pedro Espinoso and his outraged bandits would gladly undertake such a task.

"Well, boys," began Beanie, "you've heard the proposition. Now what do you want to do?"

"Take the town!" roared Helge Wahlgren, his

voice hoarse with anger. "Ve can do it und vip Montaño, too!"

"And you, *amigos?*" inquired Bogan, turning to Numero Tres and his friends. "If we attack the town, Montaño says he will kill us . . . but if not, he will take us back. What answer shall we send?"

"¡*Muchachos!*" cried out Numero Tres, springing forward to face his men, and for five minutes or more, while the Americans looked on glumly, he gesticulated and shouted in Spanish. He pointed to the brand, burned into his cheek by Bracamonte, and shook his hard fist toward the town, then he made terrible motions of men stabbed with bayonets as he denounced Bracamonte's slaying of the wounded, and, when he had ended, the excitable Mexicans declared as one man for war.

"Well, you see," said Bogan, turning to Gambolier, "these here Mexicans will be glad to have our help. And if we throw in with Numero Tres, ain't he a Mexican citizen? And then where's that filibuster stuff?"

"Hah! A mere handful of peons! An outlawed Yaqui Indian!" answered Gambolier with a scornful shrug. "But, if you like them for company . . . Montaño will kill them, too. I offer you general amnesty and two hundred dollars a month with back pay."

He stood, smiling cynically, as the adventurous Americans suddenly burst into quarrel among themselves, and then there was a shouting outside the door. The guard made way and into their midst burst the long-lost Jimmy Sullivan. He was dripping with water and his carroty red hair was plastered down to his face, and across his shoulders he carried a heavy sack.

Here's some cartridges!" He grinned, dropping the sack at Bogan's feet. "The boys sent 'em . . . to shoot in your Springfields. And you'll need 'em" he added, "because Pedro Espinoso was starting down the river when I left."

"Oh, he was, eh?" observed Bogan, grabbing up the sack of cartridges and passing them hastily around. "Say, somebody give Jimmy a Springfield."

"And my answer?" demanded Gambolier as Beanie hustled past him. "What message shall I take to Montaño?"

"Give 'im that," said Beanie, thrusting a cartridge into his hand, "and tell 'im to come and get us!"

CHAPTER SIXTEEN

The news that Jimmy Sullivan brought destroyed the last hope of peace—it was war now, and war to the knife. Jimmy had been hiding all day in the willows, begging and filching the spare cartridges of the guard while he kept a jealous eye on his enemies. Within that category he now numbered Montaño, as well as the shifty Gambolier and the gorilla-faced Pedro Espinoso, and he had greeted with unholy glee the reverses that had attended the *insurrectos*. But when, at nightfall, he saw Pedro Espinoso and his men moving stealthily off down the river, he rose up and followed after them.

Of Montaño's threats against the Foreign Legion he was fully informed by the guards, but this furtive expedition under cover of darkness meant but one thing from Prickly Pete. Rather than sack Fronteras, rather even than kill Bracamonte and throw him to the dogs in the street, Espinoso would give up his last hope of heaven for revenge on the Foreign Legion. Three times in one day he had been baffled and humiliated by them, but now, with the orders of Montaño behind him, he was marching to take them into custody. That might be difficult, while they were still at full strength, but in the morning, after they had been broken by machine-gun fire of the Federals, it would not be such a difficult task. So reasoned Espinoso as he marched down the river, but already Jimmy Sullivan with his heavy bag of cartridges was on his way to the bridge.

With enemies on all sides and the net drawing tighter that would snatch them away to prison, the Foreign Legion felt a sudden gust of joy at the desperate alternative that lay before them. To slip forth into the night and rush the town, to fight from door to door until the *cuartel* or cathedral was theirs, and then, in a glorious man to man struggle, to go down fighting against odds or be hailed the conquerors of the city! It was a vision to make them forget all else. But if his men forgot, in the joys of anticipation, Beanie Bogan most certainly did not. Behind brave Buck O'Donnell he had marched into Villa Nueva, only to be mowed down by the masked machine-guns of the Federals, and this time he laid his plans with great care.

First, he beckoned to Numero Tres and spoke to him long and earnestly before he sent him gliding off into the night, and, while he was waiting for his scout to return, he gave his orders and announced the watchword for the night. Every man was required to wear white bands on his sleeves, to prevent mistakes of identity in the dark, and the watchword that was whispered from man to man was: "Remember Buck O'Donnell!" Bogan divided his men into three separate companies, each commanded by a seasoned soldier, and, when Numero Tres came back, having located the Federal outposts, he explained his plan of attack.

"Now, here's the dope, boys," he said as they stood waiting in the half darkness, "and remember every word I say. McCafferty will stay here with his platoon of men to take care of Pedro Espinoso. Numero Tres and the Mexicans will slip down below the town and start shooting when the moon comes up, and then, when the Federals show where they are hid, the rest of us will rush the town. After that, it'll be every bunch for itself, but lay off on the drinking and the loot. We'll get no quarter if we ever get caught, so we might as well go in to win. " '*Sta bueno*, Numero Tres"—he nodded to the Yaqui—"and remember . . . *cuándo sale la luna!*"

He made a motion of the moon rising up, and the Yaqui and his warriors filed out. They were picked fighting men, each with some grievance against Bracamonte or the Federals who held the town, and they rolled their eyes at Bogan and his comrades in promise of wild work to come. The last firing had ceased, and, as they slipped off through the shadows, not a single shot gave the alarm. The white houses of Fronteras lay, dark-shadowed and deserted, abandoned by their frightened inhabitants and left unlighted by the treacherous Federals, yet somewhere on those house tops there were machine-guns and watchful riflemen, waiting silently for the expected attack.

Bogan picked up his rifle, then, exchanging grins with Big Bill, he led off through the starlit night.

To Whittle, who followed at his heels, it seemed strangely beautiful and calm, such a night indeed as a man would choose on which to end his earthly career. Already in the east there was a faint silvery glow where the moon, near its full, soon would rise, and in the black shadows of the cottonwoods, where they skulked now like lesser shadows, a mystic peace and quiet seemed to dwell. The men followed noiselessly along the bank of the causeway that led from the bridge into town, and far ahead, a dark bulk across the highway, lay the silent barricade of the Federals. Behind that solid fort of railroad ties and sandbags, the machine-guns were leveled and waiting, and, when they made their rush, as rush they must, the street would be swept with bullets. They would come, perhaps, as they had at Villa Nueva, mowing them down like standing grain, or, if Beanie should lead them unharmed through the storm, then death would take some other form. But it was there, the great consoler, whose swift, still hand had brought peace to many an aching heart.

They moved down to the low bridge where the canal crossed the road and there their progress was stopped, for some other *insurrecto*, perhaps under orders, had opened up the head gate at the dam. The ditch was full, flowing wide and deep, and Bogan cursed under his breath. He held up his hand, and, while they lay behind the bank, he crept up and inspected the bridge. It was flat and open, without railing or buttress, and he knew without a doubt that the guns of the Federals were trained to sweep its approach. It was a deathtrap, open and waiting—but Beanie was not seeking death.

He drew back and waited, and, as the moon tipped the east, a rifle shot rang out below the town. Another answered. There was a rattle, a volley, and then a machine-gun broke loose.

Spat! Spat! Hrrrrr . . . rup! it ripped, and the Americans rose for the rush. Yet still Bogan beckoned them back with his hand and crouched behind the bank. A chorus of yells rose above the fusillade, and then in a sudden outburst the shooting rose to battle height. A bugle sounded from the distant *cuartel*, dark forms flitted across the city streets, and then Bogan pointed toward the town. In the first touch of moonlight, standing clear against the sky, the house tops were dotted with men, not a man here and there but always in squads, until some officer, brandishing his sword in the air, rose up to beat them down.

"Now . . . low," commanded Beanie, and, crouching almost to the ground, he scuttled across the bridge. Whittle followed, and then another man, their khaki-colored clothes hardly showing against the road—and then they rushed for the town. A lone house gave them shelter, then the shadow of a fence, and, as firing burst out from the house tops, they plunged into a narrow *callejón*. It was a pathway, an alley, crooked and lined with low mud houses, and, as his men came rushing up behind him, Bogan charged boldly into the town. The machine-guns at the barricade broke out with a belated rattle, rifles crashed from the roofs on

both sides, but so swiftly did they pass that
Beanie had burst through a doorway before the
first bullets sought them out.

It was a two-story building, standing at the corner of a cross street much more pretentious than
the gloomy *callejón*, and, stumbling through the
darkness, Bogan ran up two stairways and
dragged himself out on the roof. Whittle followed,
his blood pounding hard, and others were close
behind. They were chuckling with joy at the suc-
cess of their venture, carried away by the madness
of the game, and with the eagerness of hunters
they shoved out their guns and joined in the general fusillade. On a house top below them, over
the ground they had just passed, was a huddle of
dark soldier forms, still firing at the last of their
men, but at the first slash of return bullets they
broke in a panic and the Americans sought out
other marks.

In the confusion of the attack, none of the Federals knew friend from foe, but with Bogan and his
men there was no doubt or uncertainty—all the
rest, the whole city, was against them. Upon roof
after roof along the *callejón* there appeared forms
with white bands on their arms, and, as the rattle
of their guns was added to the others, the Federals
broke for cover. Some dashed down the street
toward the center of the town, and some lay dead
on the roofs, but most of them ducked into the
houses beneath and crouched there to weather the
storm.

"Cease firing!" commanded Bogan, and, as
their own rifles were stilled, the noises of the night
reached their ears. From the lower part of town,

where Numero Tres and his band had started their mimic war, there was an uproar so violent and pierced with "¡*Vivas!*" as to suggest a veritable battle. But from the guardhouse by the bridge, where Big Bill and his men had remained as a reluctant rear guard, there was not a single shot, and soon, running madly, they came pounding up the alley and dodged into the houses on both sides. There was shouting to and fro, a rapid exchange of challenges, and then, leaving outposts to protect them from surprise, the legion swarmed into the big house.

Not a man was injured, although several were missing on sniping expeditions along the roofs, and the clamor was for an instant advance.

"On to the cathedral," they cried, "to the plaza . . . to the *cuartel!* To the custom house . . . and loot!"

To the custom house! That was the great cry; for a month they had heard of its hoarded treasures— of money and jewels and Chinese opium, worth more than its weight in gold.

"Come on!" yelled Jimmy Sullivan all a-quiver to begin plundering. "Who's with me . . . I'll lead the way!"

"You will not," returned Beanie Bogan, thrusting him roughly aside. "You talk like you'd took the town. What about them big guns on the top of the cathedral, if we don't get 'em covered before morning? One shell from that mortar and the inside of the custom house would be a chowder of you and your loot. No! Don't make no mistake! We take that cathedral tonight or tomorrow we go up in smoke!"

"Well, come on, then," ragged Sullivan, "hurry up! Git a move on! Them Mexicans are taking the town!"

"What Mexicans?" demanded Beanie.

"Why, Number Three and his outfit! They're damned near up to the bullring!"

"Well, good for Number Three," answered Beanie quietly, "but no Mex is going to take this town. That calls for intellect and military strategy and neither you nor a Mex has got either. We're up against artillery and dis-cip-line, and machine-guns, and all we've got is nerve and good shooting. But if you do what I tell you and keep under cover, it's an even break we win."

"Aw, I'm going!" cried Sullivan, and he was making a break for the door when a sudden blow landed him in a heap.

"You're not!" returned Bogan, taking away his gun and beckoning to two stalwart men. "You're under arrest, and the next time I hit you, it won't be no little tap!" He breathed on his knuckles and glanced about inquiringly, but no one else questioned his authority.

"Well and good," he said, "but while I'm in command, I'll speak to no buck soldier twice. Now stay where you are while I go up on the roof, and I'll lead you as far as you'll go."

The house where they were gathered was a deserted Mexican grocery, and, as Beanie scanned the city and made the rounds of his sentries, the legion got its first taste of loot. The shelves of the store were lined with canned goods—peaches and pears and roast beef and baked beans—and, when Bogan came back, he found them fully fortified to march into the jaws of death. But all was quiet now, the firing had died down suddenly, and the city lay holding its breath. Along streets and alleys lurking forms dodged and darted or plunged with alarm into doorways, but the tramp of soldiers' feet and the sound of guns and bugles had ceased as if by magic. Yet Fronteras was not taken—the wily Federals had merely re-set their traps and were waiting for the legion's next move.

They slipped out the door silently, whisked swiftly across the side street, and started for the Calle Refugio. This was the main street of the city, broad and paved and lined with stores, but as he peered up and down it from the shelter of a dark alley, Beanie Bogan backed up precipitately.

"Nah, nah," he muttered as the impetuous ones tried to crowd him. "She's too quiet . . . it don't look good to me. Say, quit your pushing . . . well, take that then, you crazy danged fool. Do you want to shove me out into that moonlight?"

The recalcitrant one this time was the Texas boy, Tight Boots, and even the blow failed to stop him. "There's the custom house," he proclaimed in a loud stage whisper, stepping daringly out into the street, and Bogan jerked him back with an oath.

"Say, stay back there, will ye?" he commanded threateningly. "There'll be no looting this night. And we'll not cross that street, custom house or no custom house. It's lighted up like day."

"Ah, go on! Make a run for it!" protested the soldiers along the alley, and Beanie threw up his hands.

"All right," he said, "if you boys don't like my

leadership, I've quit now . . . get somebody you like!"

"I'll cross it," spoke up Sullivan, advancing confidently to the street corner, but Tight Boots pushed him back.

"You will not." He laughed and darted from the darkness across the moon-struck street.

"Come on!" cried Sullivan, turning to face the eager soldiers, but they did not step out into the street. As they crowded to the curb, a machine-gun tore the night with its crash of spitting shells and Tight Boots, the dare devil, went down in a heap, shot to pieces by numerous bullets. So fierce was the storm of concentrated fire that it rolled him over and over down the street until at last it left him, a huddled heap, a lone black shadow in the moonlight.

CHAPTER SEVENTEEN

"Now you know it," spoke up Bogan as his trembling men stood staring at the body of Tight Boots, "them machine-guns were up on El Club."

"Let's git 'em," they quavered trying to shake off their terror, "let's go in and kill the last one of 'em."

"Now you're talking," said Beanie, and, leaving the grisly sight behind him, he led them, stunned and silent, through the shadows. They were chastened now by the sternest of teachers, the lightning-swift hand of death, which hovered over every street to clutch them. Tight Boots had dared to question the judgment of Sergeant Bogan, won in many a hard-fought battle, and now, without compassion for his youth and spirit, death had snatched him from their midst. Jimmy Sullivan hung his head and brushed close to the wall as they glided up dimly lighted streets and even Bruce Whittle, who thought he sought for death, turned cold and sick with fear.

They went back up the alley, flitting like ghosts across the side streets, until Bogan turned west toward El Club. The Club, that same disreputable gambling house in which Whittle had lost his poor stakes, stood but two blocks up the Calle Refugio, a two-story brick structure at the intersection of a cross street and surrounded by lower houses. From its sandbagged roof the Federal machine-guns commanded the approaches to the plaza, shooting east along the Calle Refugio and north along the intersecting street, the Calle Cinco de Mayo. The plaza itself, with its towering cathedral and bastioned prison and *cuartel*, stood on the summit of a low hill or bench of ground that rose against the sky to the west. There the soldiers were quartered with their field guns and mortars, and machine-guns on the roof of the church, but all was quiet there, for the soldiers on El Club had twice shown that they needed no help.

Being a soldier of experience, Sergeant Bogan did not overlook the fact that the plaza could dominate the town, but The Club, with its machine-guns and rattling Mausers, must be stormed and taken first. While his men still shuddered at the death of Tight Boots and made threats of speedy revenge, his mind leaped ahead to the taking of The Club and the problem of carrying the town. Creeping west along an alley, now challenged by some stray dog, now startled by a shadow that seemed suddenly to give up men, he made his way to the Calle Cinco de Mayo and peered cautiously up the street. The rising moon threw a sharp, black shadow down the middle of the pavement, but on the opposite side, where its rays were unobstructed, every rock and stick stood out.

"Nope, don't like it," grumbled Beanie, but as he was turning away, a movement caught his eye. He ducked back, and then, lying down on the ground, he thrust out his head again. In the black shadow down the street, the other way from The Club and cutting off their retreat to the river, a Mexican hat bobbed and swayed about as its owner moved cautiously toward them, and behind it appeared a second, and a third, and a fourth. At an alley where the moonlight struck across the blackness of the shadow the Mexicans stepped quickly across, and, as the touch of light revealed the guns in their hands, Bogan passed the word to his men. He was just turning back to lead a hasty retreat when the machine-guns on the El Club opened fire.

Hrrr-rap! they ripped out, and the Calle Cinco de Mayo was suddenly a hornet's nest of bullets. For the space of a minute the dust rose in the street as if invisible hands struck it up, and then as abruptly it stopped.

"*Insurrectos!*" announced Bogan, running back up the alley. "Come on, it may be Espinoso!"

He dodged down a cross street, darted across into a shadow, and plunged headlong into a house, but as the legion followed after him, butting swiftly into doorways, a voice cried after them:

"Buck O'Donnell!"

"Who's that?" challenged McCafferty who was bringing up the rear.

"*¡Socorro!*" implored the voice, and up the dark

alley came running a frightened Mexican. His hat was gone as well as his gun, but he had white bands on his arms. "¡Ai, amigos!" he wailed, and then in a torrent of Spanish he poured out his message of woe. Numero Tres had led his men up the Calle Cinco de Mayo on his way to attack the *cuartel*, and then, like the wind, the bullets had come among them and killed every man but himself.

"There's somebody alive yet!" observed Beanie grimly as a .30-30 spoke out from a roof, and then in a volley the machine-guns answered, and every man plunged back through some doorway. They crowded into darkness, into ill-smelling hovels where cats skulked and chickens fluttered and squawked, but, as the Federal gunners paused to reload their machine-guns, Sergeant Bogan stepped vigilantly out. A scattering fire from the scene of disaster showed that more than one of Numero Tres's men had escaped and the belch of flame from the roof of El Club indicated the presence of a large force of Federals. But it was a Mexican battle, with both sides under cover and shooting for general results, and Beanie grunted contemptuously. "Come on, boys," he said, "here's our chance to slip up on them. Let's go in and give 'em hell."

He started off down the *callejón*, keeping scrupulously within the shadow, and so intent were the Federals upon annihilating Numero Tres that they failed to notice his approach. Traveling by twos and threes and dodging from doorway to doorway, the legion crept closer and closer to its goal, but, as they crossed the last street, some Federal saw them running and smashed a bullet into the wall. The next group of men were greeted with a volley that filled the street with flying lead, and then the machine-guns took it up. For half an hour, while the Americans lay hidden in houses, the gunners raked the *callejón* with shot, and then the firing stopped. The old silence came back, that tense, watchful silence that falls when gunners wait for their prey, and once more Bogan ventured to look out.

With ten picked men he had led the advance, making each rush singly so that no storm of bullets could wipe them out by surprise, and now, in the lee of a protecting wall, they held a council of war.

"We're too close, boys," said Beanie after they had all expressed their views, "they can shoot right down on these roofs. We've got to get back where we can wing them gunners, and then we can rush the joint. But at the same time," he added as Sullivan began to murmur, "if they's any of you want to stay here, I've a little special work to be done."

"I'll go you!" barked Sullivan, leaping forward to claim the duty, and Bogan gave him a box of matches.

"All right," he said, "see how close you can slip up and touch a match to some old wooden shack."

"I'll burn the whole block," returned Sullivan recklessly. "You beat it and watch my smoke."

"Burn 'em one at a time then," called Bogan after him, "and don't get killed, you danged fool. And now back to the adobes, boys. We'll show 'em some night fighting that'll make 'em sorry they spoke."

He shot like a flash across the narrow street and

the bullets slashed the ground behind him. Then, as the firing died away, Whittle darted over after him, and the bullets spattered again. It was a game now, with him as with the rest of them, a game of life and death, but so surcharged with excitement that all fear and anxiety vanished. The greatest game in the world, for which all boys prepare from the moment they can dangle a sword—the game of kill or be killed! He realized now that all the rough sports he had enjoyed—the football, the boxing, the lacrosse—were miniatures of war, of that ultimate and greatest of conflicts, when men bandy bullets instead of blows. The Federals were shooting, and watching the street corners, as hunters watch a gap for deer, but soon, if Jimmy Sullivan made good his promise, there would be bullets going back.

Whittle ran down the street to catch up with Beanie, his leader in this sport of sports, and a great thankfulness came over him that he had been spared by death to be in at such a glorious finish. At the taking of a city—or another Alamo, where every man would go down fighting. On the roof of a house he lay down beside Beanie, who was building a hasty barricade, and watched him with a soldier's pride. Bogan was a master of his craft, an expert rifleman as well as a leader of men, and, as he tore loose adobes and laid them along the house top, Whittle carefully did the same. Then he lay flat behind them, his rifle thrust between, and waited for the fireworks to begin.

A glare of flames almost at the base of El Club rose up like a red tongue in the night and the Americans greeted it with a cheer, then, as the rising conflagration revealed the Federals behind their sandbags, a careful sniping began. The blaze rose up higher, turning the night into day and pointing out every brick on the building, and, as their gunners went down before the sure fire of the Americans, the Federals abandoned their posts. Shrill yells and "*¡Vivas!*" came from the Cinco de Mayo where Numero Tres and his *insurrectos* had taken shelter, and then fire after fire rose up about them as they took up the work of destruction. But here once more they defeated their own purpose, for where Bogan's fire left his men in shadow and lit up the citadel of the Federals, Numero Tres simply blinded his own fighting men and revealed their presence to the enemy.

Not 200 yards away, on the summit of the hill, stood the massive stone cathedral, and, as the swarming *insurrectos*—who had been joined by deserters from both the Federal and Montaño's camps—assembled in a side street for a charge, the machine-guns on the cathedral suddenly raked them from the side and threw them into confusion. They scattered like quail, and, as fleeing men crossed the Cinco de Mayo, the gunners of The Club, throwing caution to the winds, sprang up to mow them down. But their triumph was short-lived and man after man went down before the Federals awoke to the source of the bullets and abandoned their guns in a panic.

The roof of El Club was strewn with dead and wounded, shot down by the invisible legion, and, while the Federals on the cathedral were still cheering their victory, every gun on The Club fell silent. The ramparts were left vacant, the last head disappeared, and Bogan let out a yell. Five minutes later, with his men behind him, he went creeping up the street, and, before the Federals on the roof were aware of their presence, Helge Wahlgren came hurtling at the door. It burst in before him and the next instant the legion was there and pouring in. From one room to the other, up stairways, down cellars, they rushed with their guns ready to strike, and after one look, when they burst out upon the roof, the Federals laid down their arms.

It was theirs in a minute, without the loss of a man—The Club with its elegant private suites, its wine cellars, and its ponderous safe. There was shelter there, and treasure, and guns and ammunition, a fortress and a palace in one. From the sandbagged roof there was a stuttering tattoo as Jimmy Sullivan and a band of irrepressibles turned the machine-guns upon the church, but within The Club all was shouting and confusion as the soldiers rampaged about. In the main gaming hall, with its wheels and tables and glittering mirrors and bar, some ransacked desks and drawers, some rioted among the wet goods, and others battered and smashed at the safe. At last their dream, the dream of all soldiers, had become a glorious reality, and, they joined in a mad scramble for loot.

On the roof of El Club Beanie Bogan, the conqueror, stood gazing at the work of his hands— the buildings still burning, the dead and the wounded and the cowering Federal prisoners in the corner.

"Turn 'em loose," he said to the guard. "¡Bueno!

¡*Vamos, machachos!*" And he beckoned the Federals to go.

"No, no," they cried, tearing off their caps and coats and the hated insignia of Reyes, "we will join the *insurrectos* . . . the valiant Army of Liberation!"

"*Muy bien,* but go!" answered Bogan impatiently. "The valiant Army is camped up the river."

He hustled them outside, more dazed than ever, and entered the main gambling hall. All the lights were burning brightly, a volunteer barkeeper was nimbly mixing drinks at the bar, and the legion was there to a man.

"Hey," he shouted, rolling his eyes on them roguishly, "you're a hell of a bunch of soldiers! Do you expect me to stand guard all alone? Four men to the roof and two at each door! Come on, now, who's got the most stuff? Well, up you go, then, or I'll drumhead ye for looting! And now, barkeep, I'll have that drink."

CHAPTER EIGHTEEN

According to the Articles of War and the Hague Convention, pillage and looting are expressly forbidden, but in the bright brief lexicon of the soldier of fortune there is no dearer word than "loot." It is the reward of the conqueror, handed down from a time when war was something more than straight murder. If Sergeant Bogan had tried to restrain his wild followers in their first mad revel at The Club, he would have been as impotent as Canute on the shore of the sea when he ordered the waves to turn back. Gambolier might have attempted it, but Bogan was a top sergeant and he knew his men too well. The time had come, after days of hardship, when they had found the opportunity to relax, and the best thing to do, and the pleasantest to boot, was to throw in with the boys and enjoy it.

Outside The Club the fires burned low, the city fell back to fitful calm, but within all was shouting and drinking and excitement and trying the games of chance. Upon the hill above them some 600 Federals looked down from their stone forts in awe, from across the river and from Montaño's camp thousands of people stared across in wonder, but the gallant legionnaires, putting all fears behind them, ramped and rioted like the barbarians they were. The great Club safe was laid on its back with a *thud* that shook the town, and, while others came and went, Helge Wahlgren and Big Bill played an anvil chorus on its door. The instrument was a sledge-hammer, brought in by some bold scout, and both Helge and Big Bill were giants of strength, but Beanie Bogan refused to take any interest in their puerile attempts at safe-cracking. There was only one way, as he knew very well, of springing that ponderous door, and that was with a charge of dynamite.

The revelry was at its height when the telephone by the bar set up a persistent ringing and at last Beanie Bogan, with a braggart's flourish, took the receiver off the hook.

"Hello!" he bellowed. "Yes, good marnin' to ye! Sure, this is Sergeant Bogan himself. Have we took the town? Well, all we want of it . . . we're resting and recuperating at The Club. What's that ye want? A story for your paper? Ah, come on over and get it!"

He rang off abruptly, and for some time to come paid no more attention to the bell, until once more he did a two-step and, taking down the receiver, replied in the shrill voice of a girl.

"What's that you say?" he mimicked, while his men gave way to roars of laughter. "Oh, hello,

Pepe, how's the boy this evening? This is certainly an unexpected pleasure. Yes, Sergeant Bogan speaking. What can I do for you, General? And by the way, when are you going to have me executed?"

He crossed his legs and stood there, grinning, while he listened to the voice on the phone, and a silence came over the room. Pepe Montaño was talking to Bogan over the special wire from his camp, but, as he continued his remarks, the smile on Beanie's lips gave way to a saturnine snarl.

"Oh, you're going to take the town, are ye?" he shouted at last. "Well, we've took half of it ourselves already. Yes, the same bunch of bums that you kicked out of camp and ordered to have shot at sunrise. Oh, we don't give a damn . . . go as far as you like . . . but let me tell you one thing, Mister Montaño. Don't make the mistake of coming between us and the river. No, we don't . . . we don't recognize nothing . . . and we don't take orders from nobody. If you want to take the town, take it from the east, south, or west, but don't you cut off our retreat . . . not after what Gambolier said. And another thing, Pepe, if I get my gun on Espinoso, I'll bore him sure as hell. That's all now . . . no hard feelings . . . we'll be right here at The Club. Go to it, old boy. Ta-ta!"

He hung up the phone, and, as he turned to his men, his mouth was twisted hard.

"Well, cut it out now!" he snapped. "This has gone far enough . . . Pepe has ordered a general attack. Every man to the roof except Bill and eight more . . . and Whittle, you take charge of the bar. Barricade them doors, Bill, and put sandbags in the windows, and don't let no Mexicans in. We'll let 'em fight this out among themselves."

"And then we'll crack that safe," suggested Big Bill hopefully.

"No we won't," answered Bogan. "The first dynamite we get will go toward cracking that cathedral."

He mounted to the roof, and for an hour they lay, waiting and listening, for the first gun of the attack. Then as all remained quiet, one head after another dropped down and the wearied legion slept. In the great hall below, where Big Bill watched the door and Whittle guarded the bar, sleep crept in and conquered them, also, until at last they woke up startled and found that the day had dawned. But something had awakened them, and, as they stumbled to the windows, they heard the thunder of cannon.

"It's Long Tom!" cried McCafferty, and, as a cheer came from the roof, he turned and ran up the stairs. Whittle followed on the jump, only to find Beanie Bogan beating down inquisitive heads with his gun barrel.

"Never mind now," he said, "take my word and the rest of 'em . . . the big tank is bored through and through. And I know who did it . . . the dirty Irish Mick . . . it was little Tommy Cruse, that deserted us. Sure he's had his gun aimed for more than a week at that big black tank on the hill, and the municipal water supply is gone, the first shot. Next he'll bust the *cuartel* where Bracamonte is, or maybe it'll be the church."

They lay quiet and listened, gazing out between the sandbags at the cathedral and the houses about. The *cuartel* and jail were over the hill, concealed by the buildings between. At the foot of the slope lay the tree-grown park, where the band played in happier times, but its peace was unruffled by shot or shell. Long Tom had fired its last shot. When, later in the day, Tommy Cruse crept in and joined them, he was cursing and laughing at once—cursing Gambolier, who had insisted upon a screw breech block, and laughing at his one perfect shot. The next time it was fired, the breech block blew out and the *insurrecto* artillery was scrapped.

But the firing of Long Tom was more than an incident; it was the signal for a general assault. As the legionnaires peered and listened, they heard a faint yell, and then the distant firing of guns. It was off to the south, and a minute afterward there was a wild fusillade down the river. Then the bullets began to sing as the excited mountain Mexicans opened up from the trenches on the plain. In the early morning darkness they had surrounded the city and already they were inside the town. But along the river—on that forbidden ground the legion had claimed as its own—there were only a few stray shots from the insurgents who had retreated to the bridge.

When the sun rose on the scene, the Federals were retiring and the *insurrectos* were marching into the town, but, just as their victory seemed almost assured, there was a roar from the field gun on the cathedral and a tongue of white smoke belched out. The gun was concealed from the view of the legion by the façade that rose above the roof, but the explosion of the shell could be plainly seen as it burst above the distant *insurrec-tos*. The gun roared out again, and at the third or fourth shell the Army of Liberation broke and ran. With his usual masterly strategy, Montaño, or Gambolier, had delayed the attack till dawn, and now for the third time the wild mountaineers were stampeded by the crash of bursting shrapnel. To the south, and to the west, the guns hurled their shells, and by the time the legion had finished its breakfast, the rebels were driven from the town.

"The damned fools!" cursed Bogan bitterly as he watched the last high hats fade from sight. "They wait around all night, when they might have took the town, and charge against artillery at dawn. And now, by grab, these Federals will get cocky and shoot the holy liver out of us."

But the Federals were Mexicans, and breakfast was ready, so the legion was left in peace. They were in a perilous position, practically cut off from all retreat and almost under the guns of the *cuartel*, but already it had been shown that the Federals were deserting and had no heart for the conflict. The highly trained gunners, commanded by officers who had learned their profession in Europe, were Bracamonte's chief reliance and support, and for the moment at least he seemed very well satisfied to leave the legion alone. For not only had they routed the pick of his soldiers and fought their way up to his stronghold, but they had broken up as well certain negotiations with Montaño, looking toward the peaceful surrender of the town.

It was easy to understand the chagrin and blind envy that had prompted the *insurrecto* attack. In a moment of bravado Beanie Bogan had boasted that he had taken half the town, and to the startled Montaño, watching the glare of burning buildings, it had seemed true beyond a doubt. But what would happen to his position as a leader if the impossible should actually take place—if these turbulent Americans should storm the plaza unaided and demand the surrender of the town? Montaño knew Bogan and the desperate hardihood of his men, and he had ordered a general attack. Then, since the telephone was still in commission, he had called up the Federal colonel, Bracamonte. In his stiffest manner he gave him until daylight to raise the white flag above the *cuartel*, and then, ringing off, he sent out his army with orders to attack at dawn. No white flag had appeared, Long Tom had given the signal—but the result had made Montaño tear his hair.

Yet something must be done, the Army of Liberation must not allow itself to suffer such disgrace! Should it be whispered through Mexico that forty Americans had triumphed while they had thrice fled? Should the word go to Reyes that, while Montaño bluffed and paltered, these riff-raff had taken the town? Once more the phone rang, and, when Bogan went to answer it, a chastened voice came to his ear.

"Why, hello, *mi* General!" cried Beanie with mock cordiality. "Say, that sure was a fine piece of work! Oh, nah, nah, I don't mean your attack. My Lord, that was rotten . . . but say, didn't you hear that Long Tom hit the tank? A dead center, believe me, and the water ran out till it took all the pressure off our pipes. Yes, we're stopping at The Club . . . swell quarters, you bet . . . but what have you got on your chest?"

It is difficult, of course, for a Spanish gentleman to reply to a question like that, but Pepe Montaño knew Bogan too well to beat about the bush. "Sergeant Bo-gan," he began, "your heroic assault made my men both jealous and proud . . . jealous that Americans should be the first to storm the city but proud that you are a part of our army. The time was not ripe to begin our attack, but, when they saw the flames rising up against the sky, they clamored for an instant assault. They pictured the Foreign Legion, fighting desperately against great odds and unsupported by their comrades at arms, and so, to be brief, I ordered the attack which resulted as you saw in defeat."

"Of course it did!" broke in Beanie impatiently. "Did Gambolier lay out that attack? Well for cripes' sake, fire him! And I'll tell you something, Pepe . . . you ought to know it by this time . . . them big hats can't go up against artillery. Ah, nix on the alibis. Ain't the Foreign Legion here, right up within pistol shot of the plaza? Well, get rid of Gambolier and forget all that strategy and come in and take the town! I can tell you how to do it, and, if you don't believe me, I'll hop in and *show* you, by grab!"

"I believe you, Sergeant Bo-gan," answered Montaño, laughing jovially. "You have certainly shown us already. And that brings me to what I had to say. I have arranged a little truce with Colonel Bracamonte while we care for our wounded and dead, and he has agreed, in recognition of your valor, to let you march out with all the honors of war."

"What d'ye mean," demanded Bogan, "with all the honors of war? D'ye think for a minute we're going to quit, when we're right up next to the plaza? Well, guess again, and you'll probably be right . . . but say, this is my busiest time of day."

"Oh, no, no," protested Montaño, "don't ring off yet. I want to explain my position. Now any little thing I can do for you, Sergeant, don't hesitate to let me know. But as matters stand now, I shall be unable to assist you, and so you must come out immediately."

"All right, *mi* General," answered Beanie grimly, "I'll put that order on file."

"On file?" repeated Montaño. "Perhaps I don't understand you. But if ten thousand dollars would be any inducement. . . ."

"It wouldn't," answered Beanie. "What I need is some dynamite. You diplomats make me tired."

CHAPTER NINETEEN

Having refused for the legion the joint offer of Bracamonte and Montaño, of general amnesty and the full honors of war, Beanie Bogan posted his men to repel an attack and sent out a scouting party for dynamite. The honors of war were an empty affair, compared with the massive Club safe, and, as knowledge of the offer might detract from that singleness of purpose so desirable in a proper buck soldier, Sergeant Bogan refrained from mentioning it to his men. Instead, he indulged them by allowing the relief to hack and belt away at the safe, and the dynamite squad, searching the stores for Giant Powder, imagined they were understudies for safecrackers. But it was Beanie's purpose, when he got the dynamite, to make it into hand grenades—and, as for cracking the safe, that would be very poor generalship, for they would surely fall out over the loot.

In an ideal state the staid citizen soldiers would

scorn the mere thought of pillage, but soldiers of
fortune are a breed by themselves and seldom
deep students of philosophy. Beanie Bogan knew
his men and of one thing he was certain—the moment they accumulated any large amount of plun-
der their enthusiasm for fighting would cease. He
would have to look back to see if they were following, and no leader can do that and win. So he
prayed for dynamite, but when the scouts returned, they brought only Numero Tres. He came
in grinning, the livid 3 on his cheek showing red
against the bronze blackness of his skin, but when
Bogan mentioned dynamite, he nodded eagerly
and slipped back out the door. The hour of grace
that Bracamonte had granted expired before the
dynamite was found, and, as a scattered fire broke
out by the bridge, it was taken up all along the
river. It grew by degrees to a steady fusillade directed at the church on the hill, and then the Federal artillery replied. The firing from the river was
at too long range to have any great effect, but to the
beleaguered Foreign Legion, now threatened with
bombardment, it came as a welcome relief. The
Army of Liberation was not wholly composed of
ignorant, cowardly peons; there were men among
them who had the courage of patriots and the
fighting nerve of Americans. They had seen the legion, alone and unsupported, enter the town the
day before, and now in emulation they were
swarming down the river, shooting over the bank
as they came. A yell of encouragement went up
from El Club as they saw the first rush of high
hats, and from the guardhouse, and from the bullring, where the *insurrectos* had taken shelter, there

came an answering cheer. Then the lead began to fly and the legion crouched down and waited for the insurgents to come in.

The battle was at its height, with the Federal mortar *booming* and the volleys from behind the ditch bank gaining strength, when suddenly a band of rebels came charging across the open, and the Federal machine-guns opened up. Far in advance of the rest, made conspicuous by his red shirt, a single sturdy Mexican led the way, and, as he plunged into an adobe unscathed by the hail of bullets, the legion gave him a cheer. It was taken up by the yelling crowds of Americans who lined the north side of the river, and the *insurrectos* in the ditch, roused to heroism by his daring, leaped out and went rushing after him. Once more the spattering machine-guns tore up the earth around them and struck some of the bravest down, but the rest kept on and gained the shelter of the houses— and the honor of the army was redeemed.

On the day before there had been a street barricade to face, and the houses had been peopled by Federals, but the night raid of the legion had outflanked the barricade and cleared a whole sector of the town. The machine-guns that fired now were half a mile away, on the roofs of the cathedral and *cuartel*, and so, by what seemed a miracle to the insurgents, they escaped with a trifling loss. On they came up the streets and *callejóns,* whooping and shouting and breaking down doors, and not until they debouched upon the Calle Refugio did the machine-gun fire really tell. A sudden storm of bullets from a platoon of concealed guns overwhelmed them then, as it had poor Tight

Boots, and cut them down like grass. They retreated in a panic, but, finding the side streets
safe, they began to close in on the plaza.

The plaza at Fronteras, like all Mexican plazas,
is the center and the heart of the town. On the
west side stands the *cuartel*, a barracks and prison
in one, and opposite it the stone cathedral, on the
north the post office and municipal buildings, and
on the south the public market. The Calle Refugio
leads in from the east, a steep street fronting the
park on the south but lined with low houses on
the north. El Club, where the Foreign Legion had
taken shelter, stood just at the foot of the hill and,
having lost this citadel, Bracamonte had masked
three machine-guns on the roof of the two-story
post office.

As these masked guns spoke out from their barricades, mowing down the first of the insurgents,
the sharpshooters on the top of El Club promptly
opened on the gunners and the battle for the
heights began. But shut in as they were by the
huge heaps of sandbags that had been piled up
against every door, the legion could not join in on
this charge, even if Bogan had given the word. Yet
so closely did they shoot that all three of the
machine-guns were silenced before the *insurrectos*
advanced. On they dashed from house to house,
their enormous sombreros dotting the street as
they lost them or went down, but the bravest of
them breasted the summit of the hill, where they
wavered as if struck by a wind. From the flat roof
of the *cuartel* with its towers and embrasures a
hailstorm of bullets swept the street and hundreds
of Federals, lying safely behind its walls, for the

first time entered the fray. They were Bracamonte's reserves, gathered in from trench and outpost and posted thickly for the defense of the plaza.

The insurgents fell back, leaving their dead and wounded to sprawl and struggle in the street, and sought shelter in the lower part of the town. There, north of the hill but clinging to its base, lay the famous Calle Diablo, the crooked Devil's Street that housed the combined vice and wickedness of the city. But as the first wave of *insurrectos* was lost in its deadfalls, a second came to take its place. In the heat of the conflict the approaches had been left open and others had rushed into the town. They came hurrying down the river in tens and twenties, drawn on by the sounds of battle, and others, even more bold, waded across from Del Norte and joined, unarmed, in the assault.

The second wave came on up past El Club, where the Americans were covering their advance, and, as they ducked into the buildings across the street from the church, a tremendous explosion rent the air.

"Dynamite," yelled Bogan as a cloud of yellow smoke rose up from the garden of the church, "by grab, I wish I could get a few sticks!"

On the roof of a house a big Mexican appeared, whirling a sputtering ball in a sling, and, as he let it go, sling and all, through the air, it burst against the wall of the church.

"That's the stuff!" cheered Beanie from behind his rampart. "Swing 'em high and put one on the roof! Oh, Lord, they got 'im! And there's another one down! I could show 'em a few things about bombing!"

One after the other, with daredevil recklessness, the *insurrectos* leaped into the open and hurled their bombs at the church, but in the concentrated fire of the machine-guns the hand grenade men went down, and then, as the explosions ceased, a yell went up from the plaza. The next moment a line of charging men came dashing over the brow of the hill and made for the battered houses. It was the troop of Federal *rurales*, the picked fighting men of Mexico, which had been quartered there since the siege of Fronteras, and at sight of their high hats and flashing carbines the *insurrectos* turned and fled. For a generation and more the gaudy uniform of the *rurales* had spelled terror and death to all Mexicans, and the Calle Diablo swallowed up the last of the bold bombers. The mortar opened up on the river and the bullring and the backbone of the assault was broken.

Yet if the Mexicans had finished, the Irish had not, for in the rear of the second rush Numero Tres had come running with a heavy box of dynamite on his back.

"From General Montaño!" he announced with a smile. "He sends his compliments to Sergeant Bo-gan!"

"Oho!" exclaimed Bogan as he tore open the box. "Well, go back and ask for some more. And tell him from me that, if he'll give me enough powder, I'll level that hill off as flat as a Mexican tortilla. Now cut up these sticks, boys, and stuff 'em into cans . . . I'll tend to the caps and fuse. We've hid out long enough, and, if we don't stop them *rurales*, they'll have us backed up against a wall. Now, Bill, you take your boys and go up on the roof and pick off every *rurale* that shows, and Whittle and the rest of us will get into them houses and shoot our way through with dynamite. Bring along those crowbars . . . we'll have to dig through the walls and start out when I blow up the first house."

He hustled to the roof and looked up at the *rurales*, who were advancing from house to house down the hill, and then, with an oath, he ran down the stairs and went scuttling across the street. With his arms fall of bombs Whittle followed closely behind him, and, before the Federals had discovered their maneuver, they had burst into a deserted house. It was a one-story adobe, the first of the long row that extended in a line up the hill, and, once inside, Bogan laid aside his gun and picked up a dynamite bomb.

"Now watch me clean 'em," he said to Whittle, and slung the can of powder in a cloth. Then, pushing open the back door so he could get a full, right-hand swing, he drew on his cigar, applied the end to the short fuse, and stood waiting to make his throw. The fuse sputtered and spit back and Bogan stepped to the door, then, leaping boldly outside, he whirled it in the air and sent it hurtling over the flat roofs of the houses. It fell, and the next instant the ground shook beneath them with the force of the terrific explosion. The house they were in seemed to leap and bulge with the kick of the great wave of air, and, as a great silence fell, Bogan peeped out the door and jerked his head back, grinning.

"That'll hold 'em!" He laughed. "The whole

roof's busted in! And here come the rest of the boys!"

He ran to the front door as the remainder of his squad came rocketing in from the street, and an outburst of firing from the roof of The Club gave notice that Big Bill was on the job. Bogan seized a steel bar from one of the men and struck it into the mud wall of the house, and then, as the bullets *thudded* harmlessly against their shelter, the legion began to dig. Like Thor of old, Helge Wahlgren swung a sledge-hammer until he battered a huge hole in the wall, and, as they poured through the breach, they attacked the next wall until they had tunneled their way to the wreck. Where once had been a roof, overlaid with heavy brush and plastered with a foot of solid mud, the hewn rafters were broken and smashed to the ground by the force of one tomato can of dynamite. And buried in the ruins they found three *rurale* hats to show where their owners had fled.

"That's the stuff!" exclaimed Bogan, gloating over the wreckage. "Now watch this, boys, and see how it's done."

Once more he lit a fuse and watched it with steady nerves until it had burned close down to the bomb, and then, ginning wickedly, he whirled it outside the door and sent it flying over the houses beyond.

Boom! it thundered, and, as the *rurales* broke from cover, Big Bill and his sharpshooters shot them down.

"Now, quick work," yelled Bogan, "before they get onto us and go to passing some shrapnel shells back! Bust a hole in here, Helge, and you that ain't working keep an eye out, so we don't get surprised!"

He gathered up the bombs and rigged another sling out of the leg of an old pair of trousers, and, as the battle raged outside, to the beat of Helge's hammer, he burst into a crooning song.

> O-o, red-headed Nora O' Grady.
> I kissed her and called her me darlint
> O-oh, freckle-faced, red-headed Nora O' Grady
> I kissed her and called her me darlint.

He glanced up at Whittle and stopped abruptly, but the wild tune was running in his brain.

"This is living, boys!" he shouted. "Real fighting . . . you can't beat it! By Judas, we got 'em on the run.

> O-oh, snaggle-toothed, freckle-faced, red-
> headed . . .

He paused again in his perfidious chant, but, as they burst into another house, he went on with his fighting song. And the Irish about him fell to rollicking with joy as they sensed the significance of their conquest. Not an hour before two companies of *insurrectos* had attacked this same hill and fallen back, but they, with the battle-wise Bogan to lead them, were driving steadily on toward the plaza. Except for the fact that it would draw the enemy's fire, they could easily snipe the Federals from the church and, with every bomb clearing four or five houses at a time, they would soon be

up to the plaza. Then the fight would begin, the
battle royal that would put the city into their
hands, and make them masters of northern Mexico. What would Montaño say then—and Gambolier and Espinoso—would they concede that
the legion could fight? They would that and more,
and for every low trick they had suffered the Irish
would have their revenge.

A shout from El Club and then a fusillade of
shooting marked the final panic-stricken flight of
the *rurales*, and, as they darted across the plaza and
into the *cuartel*, the sappers and miners joined the
cheer. But after their yell, there came another and
another from the region of the Calle Diablo, and
then with a roar that shook the ground a great
bomb went off behind the post office. Frightened
Federals came flying like birds out of a tree from
the wracked and splintered building, and, as the
legion stared and listened, they saw smoke rise up
and heard the crackling of flames.

Then a great belch of fire rose up to the skies
and the earth trembled from bomb after bomb. It
was the beaten *insurrectos*, returning to the conflict and storming the hill from the north, and at
every explosion Beanie Bogan gave a howl and
urged his sappers on.

CHAPTER TWENTY

Beneath a cloud of smoke that darkened the sun and shielded them like a banner from their enemies, the Foreign Legion took to the open at last and charged to the corner of the plaza. A great tongue of flame was licking the skies as the interior of the post office took fire, and not far from its brick walls the legion found a refuge on the roof of the municipal hall. As the conflagration raged on, the Federals ceased firing and gazed at the destruction in awe, and from the Calle Diablo and the river beyond the Army of Liberation came pouring in. By every sign by which men presage such events the fall of the city seemed at hand, yet Bogan, the war-wise, sent back more men for cartridges and sandbagged his roof with care. The post office was burning, but the Federals were not whipped; they were crouching behind the walls of the *cuartel* and cathedral and Bracamonte would not let them surrender.

As the legion lay watching, a counter assault began suddenly on the slope behind the *cuartel* and soon along Calle Diablo the *insurrectos* came fleeing back. Street fighting sprang up, with men standing behind buildings and shooting at random around the corners, and then, as the Federals turned back from their sally, their mortars dropped shells on the town. But their aim was poor and the insurgents, encouraged, crept forward from house to house until they swept the plaza with bullets. The fire roared and crackled, smoke swhirled down the street or rose in a black column to the skies, and, as neither side succeeded in gaining the advantage, the legion settled down to straight sniping. Already the machine-guns on the low roof of the *cuartel* had been abandoned by their decimated crews and as his cartridges arrived—with the compliments of Montaño—Bogan gave his sharpshooters *carte blanche*. Their rifle fire quickened, the *cuartel* windows were deserted, and at last there came a lull in the Federals' shooting and a white flag appeared at the door.

"Cease firing!" ordered Bogan, and, as the flag advanced, they saw that it was borne by an American. He stepped out into the open, holding a white handkerchief above his head, and the legion burst out in a great cheer. The men slapped each other on the back, whooping and laughing with joy and shouting that the Federals were whipped, but, as the man crossed the plaza and came into view, it was seen he carried a bucket.

"Ah, surrender nothing!" cursed Bogan as they stared at him doubtfully. "Can't you see he's just going to the fountain? The greasers are out of water!"

As they peered out through their loopholes, a lugubrious silence came over the mercurial legion, and then Bruce Whittle cocked his gun. His face went white, and, as Bogan turned at the click, he saw an insane glare in his eyes.

"Look," he muttered, "look who that man is."

Bogan looked—the man was Pedley.

"Why, the son-of-a-bitch!" he burst out vindictively as he recognized the bedraggled American, and then he glanced across at Whittle. There was a world of meaning in his glinting green eyes, but Whittle shook his head.

"Then I will," urged Bogan, but Whittle shook his head again.

"No!" he said. "Don't touch him . . . let me think. He's under a flag of truce."

"Never mind about that," hissed Began in his ear, "but bean him, before he gets back."

Pedley had dipped his bucket into the basin of the fountain and was starting back to the *cuartel* but Whittle did not stir. A great rage had swept over him, submerging his reason and impelling him to shoot the man down, and then in an instant he was hot with shame at the murder that had risen in his heart. Yet here was his enemy, in the hands of the Federals, sent out through the flying bullets for water. Who would know, if one struck him down? Wild thoughts took hold of him; he glanced about uneasily, and there was Bogan, watching. Yes, Beanie would know, and he himself would know. But—perhaps a stray bullet might strike him. They began skittering across the plaza like playful locusts as the disgruntled *insurrectos* opened fire. Surely, among them all, there would be some *gringo* hater who would kill him before he escaped. For he hated him, he could not deny it, and, if God so willed, he prayed that the bullet might come. Had he not exposed his breast to the gunfire of the Federals to put his love to the test? Then why should he be concerned if Broughton Pedley went down, at last, before some bullet? Let God be their judge, then, and whichever one was left—let him go back to Constance.

But if God looks down upon each petty man and judges his fevered thoughts, he forgave Broughton Pedley for his craven fear and Bruce Whittle for his wickedness. A party of *insurrectos* in a brick building on the corner cut loose, as Pedley turned back to the *cuartel*, and, as the bullets struck about him, he threw down his bucket and ran for the shelter of the doorway.

"The dirty coward!" exclaimed Bogan indignantly. "Why the devil didn't I pot him. Hey, but look . . . he's coming out again!"

Pedley came out with a leap, impelled by a bayonet in the hands of a vicious Federal, and, as he ran toward the fountain and snatched up his bucket, the *insurrectos* began to hoot. The sniping and man-killing were forgotten for the moment in the presence of this drama of fear, and Federal and *insurrecto* laid aside their hate to see what the outcome would be. Here was a captive American, driven out by the Federals until he should return with his bucket of water, and he, poor wretch, jumping and starting at every dust puff as he scuttled unwillingly toward the fountain.

"Hey, how about this?" demanded a soldier of Bogan's. "Do we let him get that water? They're out, the suckers, and, if we keep 'em from getting any. . . ."

"Never mind now," answered Bogan, squinting an eye down his gun barrel, "I'll tend to this greaser myself . . . and to think of him being an American!"

He guttered in his throat as he drew a fine bead and watched the slinking Pedley, and then, just as Pedley turned back with his water, he shot the bucket out of his hand. A whoop of derision rose up from the Mexicans as they witnessed this grim soldier's jest, and, as Pedley fled, they joined in the horseplay by tearing up the plaza with bullets. Even the Federals laughed, although they had lost their water, and the Foreign Legion roared. Then with their animosity cooled, and their curiosity whetted, they settled down to watch the *cuartel* door. It was a deeply indented entrance, flanked on both sides by brick buttresses cut with loopholes for the soldiers within, and every *insurrecto* rifle was trained on the pathway to make the *gringo* do a devil's dance.

"¡Ven! ¡Ven!" they called, but the *gringo* did not come, and at last there stepped out—a woman.

She held a bucket in each hand, and, without even hurrying her pace, she walked down the path toward the fountain. Beanie Bogan dropped his gun, Whittle rose to a crouch; the woman was Constance Pedley. Whittle gazed at her, fascinated, then he sank slowly down, and, when he looked again, she was at the fountain. The bullets had stopped, not a gun was fired, and, when she turned back, they cheered. Americans and *insurrectos* and Federals alike paid their tribute to her nerve and

courage, and then the firing was renewed. But it
was not the same battle, the *insurrectos* were shooting wildly, and the legion shot only at the church.
There was a woman in the *cuartel*, an American
woman, and any glancing shot might kill her.

As for Whittle, he drew back and started down
the stairs, but Bogan plucked him back at the door.

"Where you going?" he demanded brusquely,
and then he listened with compassionate calm.
"Yes," he said, when Whittle had finished, "that
is certainly a peach of an idee. Just the minute
you get where you can do something for your
lady, you step out into the plaza and get killed.
Oh, yes, I know you love her, and all that, and
you want to run right over there and rescue her,
but here, listen to me now . . . they's such a thing
as head work. You're plain off your noodle, to tell
you the truth, but I ain't. I've got it all figured
out. The Pedleys were in Fronteras when this
trouble broke out and the Federals throwed 'em
into jail for safekeeping, and, now their water
tank has got a big hole in it, they're using 'em to
get a little water. But that woman is just as safe
walking across the plaza as she would be on Or-
ange Grove Avenue. Nobody's going to hurt her,
she's too good a sport, but if we storm the *cuartel*
and try to rescue her, it's ten to one she gets
killed. No, we tackle the cathedral, which is as
full of Federals as hell is of cowards like Pedley,
and, if we rout them out and stop those machine-
guns, the *cuartel* will surrender of itself. And then
we'll go in and get her."

"But that may be too late!" cried Whittle wildly.
"You don't understand what I'm after. I want to

rescue her first, so we can blow up the *cuartel* and kill every man that's in it. That wouldn't be like shooting him . . . he'd go down with the rest and . . . well, he tried to do as much for me."

"Yes, and he'll try again," answered Bogan encouragingly, "until one of you takes the count. So if he comes out again . . . you just look the other way, and I'll bore him where his suspenders cross. I'm no Sunday school kid, it won't worry me none, and he's such a cowardly damned dog it's a disgrace to have him around."

Bogan spoke with the rough directness of a soldier the better to hold Whittle to his purpose, but once more he was doomed to disappointment. Whittle was indeed out of his head, harassed with anxiety for the safety of his beloved, and yet torn with indecision regarding Pedley. He sobered down suddenly at Bogan's crude words and the reason crept back into his eyes.

"Oh, no!" he burst out. "I . . . I must be sort of flighty. But you mustn't take advantage of that. I'm a gentleman, Beanie, and it would disgrace me forever to so much as wish he was dead. No, I wanted to die . . . that's the reason I came down here . . . but I wanted to do it for her. You understand, I know, because you're not as rough as you pretend to be. I'd like to die trying to save her. There's no use to live, you can see that yourself, because he's hiding in behind there while she's doing his work . . . and cowards like that never die."

"I don't know about that," observed Beanie dryly, and Whittle caught the thought behind his words.

"No, now, Beanie," he begged, "I want you to promise . . . I want you to give me your word.

Whatever happens, I want you to promise me that you won't raise a hand to injure him."

"Uhn-uh," grunted Bogan, "what's a buck soldier's promise? And what are you going to promise me?"

"Oh, anything you want," answered Whittle abjectly, "but I'd die if I made you a murderer . . . I'd rather go and kill him myself."

"Well, all right, then," agreed Bogan with a cynical grin, "but you've got to promise me to stay under cover until I tell you to come out. But if you'll do that, like a gentleman, I'll give you my word, as a soldier, not to raise my hand against Pedley. Come on now, there's something doing. I've got to get up on the roof again. Will you give your word for mine?"

"But you don't seem to mean it . . . you don't seem to care, Beanie. Now, tell me, there isn't any trick?"

"No, you bet there isn't," declared Bogan vehemently. "I was thinking about the lady. But come on now, how about it . . . will you promise if I will? Well, all right then . . . never mind, we don't need to shake hands on it . . . but you stay down here where you won't get shot."

He was halfway up the stairs when Whittle sprang after him. "No, let me come up!" he begged. "I want to be where I can see her."

"You go back there!" ordered Bogan. "And if you don't keep your promise . . . well, what can you expect, then, of a soldier?"

CHAPTER TWENTY-ONE

When Bogan reached the roof, he found his men in a turmoil and a white flag flying above the *cuartel*.

"They've surrendered!" he yelled, but his men shook their heads and pointed across the plaza. Up the long, wide street that led in from the south a man was riding in with a white flag, and a glance at the golden sorrel horse told Bogan that it was Pedro Espinoso. He came on at a gallop, holding the flag above his head, but it was certain he did not intend to surrender. It was an offer of parley, to give terms to the garrison and demand the surrender of the town. But, whether acting for himself or for General Montaño, the result would be the same—the Foreign Legion, after winning to the plaza, would be deprived of its just reward. Bracamonte would surrender to a brother Mexican and the nation would be saved from disgrace. For if the Federal army, invincible against the *insurrectos*, should surrender to forty soldiers of fortune, what Mexican was there left who could hold up his head in the presence of the fighting Americans?

Beanie Bogan took in the situation at a glance—Bracamonte had telephoned for terms to Montaño, and Montaño was sending in Espinoso to snatch away their prize.

"Shoot down that white flag, boys," he said to his sharpshooters, and, as Helge and Big Bill and the pick of his marksmen drew down on the flag above the *cuartel*, he sent a bullet skittering along the street to turn back Espinoso. But Prickly Pete was bold and headstrong, and, still carrying the flag of truce, he rode up to the door of the *cuartel*. Bogan shot at him twice, and, as Espinoso reined in, he aimed once more at the flag stick and knocked it out of his hand.

"Git, you *pelado!*" roared Bogan across the plaza, and, holding his gun low, he pumped a series of bullets in dangerous proximity to his enemy. The beautiful sorrel flew back and whirled as Espinoso bellowed back his curses, and then, at a jerk from its infuriated master, it went *clattering* away down the street. The peace conference was over, and, as the Federals opened up, Bogan emptied his gun after Espinosa. Then the legion settled down to a measured sniping, and the sun set in a pall of smoke. On the roof of the church a solid line of men shot at random over the sandbags on the wall, and the Americans, shooting back through almost invisible loopholes, searched out every opening and crack. And then, as the burning post office ignited other buildings and lighted up the plaza like day, Bogan saw Constance Pedley come out of the *cuartel* again and go to the fountain for water. A curse moved his lips as he watched the stray bullets hit spitefully into the dust about her and he glanced up to find Whittle beside him, looking down with fearful eyes.

"Won't you let me go down there?" he whispered. "I could save her . . . I know I could."

"You could not," returned Bogan, and yanked him roughly down.

"Yes, I could!" insisted Whittle. "I've got it all planned out . . . and I'm going to do it, anyhow."

"Oh, you are, hey?" remarked Bogan. "Well, what's the big idee? I suppose you've forgot all about that promise?"

"I've forgotten about everything," answered Whittle fiercely. "All I want is to strike one blow. I can't stand here idle and see her risk her life and not make an effort to save her. Listen, I've made a big bomb, and, the next time she leaves the *cuartel*, I'll rush up and throw it in at the door, and then . . . then I'll run out and take her in my arms and shield her from the bullets."

He broke down, half weeping, and Bogan bit his lip as he looked out into the night.

"Well, all right, boy," he said at last, "you get your chance . . . and the legion will be behind you. We don't amount to a damn, and, if some of us get killed, maybe she'll remember us in her prayers. We'll storm the *cuartel* when you blow down the gate . . . and you look after the woman."

He rose up silently and went down the stairway, nodding approvingly as Whittle outlined his plans, and, when at last he saw him disappear down an alley, he went back and ordered his men. The time was propitious for striking a sudden blow and perhaps it was all for the best. Already the remaining *insurrectos*, under cover of darkness, had advanced into the outskirts of the town and heavy firing in the east and south indicated a general attack in force. Like a beacon light for all to see, the flames from the burning post office warned the *insurrectos* that the legion was winning. They would press hard that night to push back the Federals and be in at the fall of the town, and the Federals, on the other hand, would draw off every man who could be spared from the defense of the *cuartel*. The garrison would be weak, Whittle's bomb would stampede them, and a rush would do the rest.

As the time went by and the fighting grew hotter, the legion became restive and distraught, and to appease their clamor Bogan detailed a squad of dynamiters to make a simultaneous attack upon the church. Another squad he compelled by oaths and threats to keep up the fire from the roof, and then with the rest he stood behind the door and waited for Constance to appear. As the blaze from burning buildings leaped and bellied before the wind, the plaza flickered with deceptive light and shadows, and men crowded to barred windows and peered out through cracks and bullet holes, to be the first to see her come.

Like a woman in a dream, unmindful of bullets or the turmoil that was to spring up about her, Constance stepped out at last from the doorway of the *cuartel* and started across the plaza. From his hiding place up the square Whittle watched her to the fountain, and then, lighting the spare fuse that was to serve as his torch and hugging the great bomb to his breast, he dashed out and down the street. Along the front of the *cuartel*, with its iron-barred windows and loopholed buttresses by the gate, he passed so quickly that not a shot was fired, and then, as a machine-gun on the church opened up at random, he plunged into the darkened doorway. Across the entrance, as he knew, there stretched a great wrought-iron grille, two huge barred gratings, that were hung from the walls and padlocked against a post in the middle. At the foot of this post he dropped his bomb, and, as the startled sentries opened fire and fled, he held his spitting torch to the fuse and ran for his life out the doorway.

There was a yell of terror from the *cuartel* behind him, and then the bomb exploded. A belch of air seemed to lift him from his feet, his ears were deafened by the crash, and, as the great flash of powder gave way to semidarkness, a shower of broken fragments fell about him. He was halfway across the plaza when, from over behind the church, another explosion ripped the night, and, as bomb succeeded bomb, throwing the Federal gunners into confusion, Beanie Bogan and his fighting legion charged. Not a cheer was given, but, in pairs and bunches and with belated men trailing behind, they came tearing across the plaza, heads up, guns pumping, like khaki-colored ghosts in a race. A scattered fire from the roof of the church failed to strike down a single man, and, as Whittle turned to watch them, he saw the leaders go bounding into the doorway. Against the glare of spitting guns within he could see their burly shoulders heave as they threw aside the shattered gate, and then they burst in and rushed the garrison, which had retreated to the rear of the *cuartel*.

A mêlée followed, so tragic in its noises that he shrank away from the sound—yells of terror, shouts of triumph, and rifles breaking out in savage shootings. Yet if his soul revolted at such bloody-handed riot, another battle had sprung up across the plaza that was as terrible in its way as the first. Along the top of the church roof, guns were flashing like fireflies, and, hurled from the street, he saw a lighted bomb mount up and explode against the massive wall. Another and another swung up from the adobe houses where Bogan's dynamite squad had taken shelter, and then from the roof there came a spitting shrapnel shell that burst with a tremendous report. It was a matching of stupendous forces forged by man for his own destruction, and in the glow of burning buildings the soldiers darted about like vengeful devils loosed from hell. He moved on in a daze hardly knowing what he sought until, against the base of the fountain, he saw a fleck of white. Then he remembered her poignantly and his heart stood still—could it be that Constance had been killed?

He rushed toward the spot and gathered her into his arms while the noise seemed to recede and die away. There was nothing else in the world but this woman that he loved, and, his hand against her heart, he drew her closer and, dipping water from the fountain, dashed it over the edge into her face, while all the time he scanned her white waist for the blood spot he feared to find. But her heart was still beating, and, as he spoke her name, she stirred and opened her eyes.

"Are you hurt?" he asked. "You must have been hit . . . I found you here on the ground."

"No," she sighed, and then something in his voice roused her up from her deadly apathy. "Why, who are you?" she cried, rising up and staring into his face. "You aren't . . . oh, are you Bruce?"

"Yes, I'm Bruce," he said, and all the tenderness of his lost and thwarted love went out to her with a rush. He drew her to him as if she were his own and kissed her again and again, while she clutched him in her arms and wept. "I'm so happy," she breathed, "so happy . . . he told me you were dead. No, don't draw away from me . . . I'm not his wife. I never was, except before the law. I couldn't be, after you kissed me, there at the end of my wedding . . . not after I knew you loved me. I've followed you everywhere to tell you. But why didn't you come, Bruce, after you had saved me from drowning? I waited for you day after day, and sometimes I thought that it was all just my fancy and that you didn't really love me at all. And then my wedding day came and . . . I was a fool, I married him . . . but it's just a bad dream now."

He kissed her again and sat holding her in his arms while the battle raged on about them. Stray bullets zipped past, tiny dust jets leaped up suddenly like mischievous elfin sprites, but, crouched in the shelter of the shelving fountain, they talked of nothing but the miracle called love.

Chapter Twenty-Two

The capture of the *cuartel* was speedily accomplished after the first fierce struggle was decided, and, as the legion poured in, the defeated Federals fled back through the corridors and escaped. Only the wounded remained, and the prisoners in the cells, and the deserting Federals who had hidden from their officers. These came out cheering, stripping off their hated uniforms and shouting—"*¡Viva* Montaño!"—and, as their surrender was accepted, they promptly joined with the *insurrectos* in breaking down the doors of the cells. A large body of *insurrectos* that had been fighting from other buildings followed close on the legion's charge, and soon the *cuartel* roof was lined with yelling Mexicans—high-hatted Chihuahuans, Federal deserters in their blankets, and prisoners in any clothes at all. But each had a gun and a hat full of cartridges, which he promptly shot off at the moon.

Freedom had dawned at last for each and every one of them and their joy was unrestrained by Beanie Bogan. He understood Mexicans, and, as a short, red-shirted *insurrecto* came bounding into the *cuartel*, he made him his lieutenant on the spot. The red-shirted Mexican was Rico Puga, the hero of the morning's charge, and then, when Numero Tres appeared, he ordered the two of them to station every Mexican on the roof. That cleared the patio and the numberless rooms that surrounded this inner court, and, placing a guard at the back and front entrances, Bogan quickly set the *cuartel* in order. Then, as he received reports on the killed and wounded, he suddenly remembered his partner.

Not since he had seen him go running across the plaza had Bogan set eyes on Whittle, and what about the girl? Cursing himself roundly for this heartless neglect, he turned over the command to Big Bill and rushed out across the plaza. The Federals on the church were fully engaged with the dynamite squad and a swarm of *insurrectos,* but the plaza was still spattered by a rain of spent bullets from the fighting going on in the suburbs. When from a distance Bogan saw dim forms by the fountain, he dashed forward with his heart in his mouth. But something about their pose suddenly stopped him in his stride, and he stood staring in frank astonishment.

"Come on into the *cuartel!*" he shouted angrily as Whittle rose up to meet him, and, when they had passed through the battered gateway, he stopped at an open door. "Give the lady this room," he ordered, and pulled down his lip reproachfully.

"All right," said Whittle, but, as Bogan turned away, he caught him by the arm. "This is Constance," he said, his voice vibrant with happiness, and Bogan bowed stiffly as he deftly struck Whittle aside.

"Well, take care of her, then," he shot back over his shoulder, and hurried away down the patio.

The room was the office of the commander of the *cuartel*, now doubtless out street fighting in the lower part of town, and, as they closed the door on the rude sights and noises, the silence fell like a benediction. The firing on the roof was like the tapping of a whip on an outstretched piece of cloth and the bloodthirsty yells of the victorious *insurrectos* sounded faint and far away. They stood for a minute, each gazing at the other with wondering, love-hungry eyes, and then without a word they drifted together and their lips met devoutly in a kiss.

Theirs was not a love such as comes to most, built up by degrees and tracing its beginning to a thousand hidden causes; they had met in the sea, battling to save their lives, and their love had sprung forth, full-grown. Then their ways had parted, misunderstandings had come between them, and she had married before she knew. But in spite of it all they were true lovers still, although the whole world might stand between. The past was less than nothing, the future might never come—they had plucked this brief moment from the wreck of their two lives and they pledged their devotion in a kiss.

Outside their door, soldiers raced to and fro, the *clang* of a sledge-hammer told where men already free were breaking open the cells of other prisoners, but in this lull of the storm that had swept them far away they sat down together to unravel, if they could, the tangled skein of their lives.

"How did you come here?" he asked, still regarding her worshipfully. "I know you are not afraid, because we saw you carrying water, but Fronteras is no place for a woman."

"No," she answered, and then she sat silently until at last she met his eyes. "You mustn't mind," she said, "if I speak about . . . him. And can you forgive me for being so weak as to marry him? Because I hate the very thought of it. Oh, I . . . but what's the use? You know I never loved him. It was arranged, in a way, but the moment he married me, he thought he could dominate my life. He thought he owned me because I had said yes and signed my name, but I left him . . . when you kissed me and ran away . . . and I've been seeking for you ever since."

"Yes," he said, "but you must know why I did it. I thought it was too late. And when I saw you in Del Norte, with him close behind. . . ."

"Yes, yes, I know. I knew what you thought and I tried every way to get word to you, but he followed me like a keeper, he even hired detectives to watch me. Then he came back one night with his face all disfigured, and somebody told me you had done it, but he sat off by himself, and by his eyes I knew he was laying some plan to kill you. He isn't the man that I thought at all . . . something has changed him and made him a brute . . . and at last he disappeared, until yesterday morning, he came back and said you were here. He said he had captured you and delivered you to the Federals to be executed for blowing up those bridges . . . and, of course, you did do it . . . but I hired a carriage and hurried over to try to save you. But that made him angry . . . angrier than anything I had done . . . and he followed after me and ordered me home, and then very suddenly the battle began and no one could cross the bridge."

"And so you were caught?" prompted Whittle.

"Yes, and put into jail . . . the Mexicans were very much excited. They thought I was your wife because I had come to plead for you, and they abused him for being an American. I could hear them talking about the *gringos*, and some of them threatened to kill him, but the commandant gave me a room by myself. Then the water gave out and the officer in charge seemed to think that the Americans were responsible. He took us from our cells and talked and gesticulated, and finally, when the wounded began to suffer for water, they ordered . . . him . . . to go out to the fountain. You must have seen it . . . the way he ran away from the bullets." She clenched her hands and stared straight ahead. "I was ashamed," she said. "I didn't know he was such a coward."

"Coward," echoed Whittle. "Well, you should have heard Beanie talk when he let them send you out in his place."

"They didn't send me," she corrected. "I volunteered to go . . . and then they ordered him to be taken back and shot."

"Shot!" cried Whittle, and, as his tense muscles relaxed, he turned and glanced at her furtively.

"Did . . . did they do it?" he asked, trying to keep his voice steady, and she flashed back an anguished look.

"I don't know," she answered, and in the painful silence they sat with their eyes on the floor. "They threatened him with death, that was why he went at first, but after the bucket was shot from his hand . . . he wouldn't go out any more."

"And you?" he questioned.

"I went for the water," the said, "and, when I came back, he was gone."

He stirred uneasily and glanced toward the doors, and at last he got up and went out. The firing from the roof had practically ceased and the shooting from the church had lulled, but, as he stood listening in the patio, he could hear the rattle of the machine-guns in the lower part of the town. The Federals were still fighting and, if they beat back the *insurrectos*, might even return and lay siege to the *cuartel*. But the tide of this battle was less to Whittle than that of another which raged in his breast, and, as he passed down the arcade, glancing furtively at prostrate bodies, he moved by some instinct in the shadows. He was searching for Pedley, and, following his own wishes, he sought first among the dead.

But Pedley was not there, either among the dead or wounded, and, while the guards looked on curiously, Whittle got a lantern and began a room to room search. It was the suspense that oppressed him, that and the vision of Constance sitting alone with her terrifying thoughts, and he started as if shot when, as he hastened from room to room, he heard a voice behind him. He whirled and there, rising up from beneath some sacks, was the man he feared to find. His coat and hat were gone, some soldier had stolen his shoes, and his round body had shrunk until his flapping clothes seemed those of some other man. He stood, crouched and trembling, his voice breaking with self-pity as he began some incoherent supplication, and then, as he recognized the man before him, his eyes bulged in a hard, triumphant stare. A sickening sense of guilt had come over Whittle as he gazed at this man risen from the dead, and, as Pedley stepped toward him, he turned in horror and fled away down the corridor. With sudden boldness Pedley followed him, as harmless snakes pursue those who flee, and, as Whittle hesitated and passed by Constance's door, Pedley turned by some instinct and entered. With a bound Whittle flew back and snatched the door open—she had risen and was facing her husband. If she was startled and did not show it, there was nothing in her eyes but a look of infinite contempt, but as Whittle came in and she met his glance, she buried her face in her hands.

"Ah, I thought so," observed Pedley, turning to leer at Whittle. "You two have been here together."

"Yes," answered Whittle, and stood irresolutely while his heart thumped against his breast.

"Well, I may as well tell you," began Pedley deliberately, "that you are both making a great mistake. I will never begin suit for a divorce. I love Constance too dearly to consent to part with her, and besides. . . ."

"You love my money!"

She added the words quickly with a flash of scorn that turned his swollen cheeks a dull red.

"And besides," he continued, "I have my honor to consider. She is my wife and no man shall take her from me."

"I am not your wife," she flared back, but her voice trailed off into a sob.

"Yes you are, dear," he replied, "and I shall never give you cause to bring action for annulment or divorce. In fact," he went on with a touch of malice in his voice, "I think this little farce may as well be closed. Much as I appreciate your solicitude for my welfare and health, I must ask you, Mister Whittle, to withdraw."

A twinge of pain swept over Whittle's pale face as he felt the cruel lash of this jest, but he turned his eyes to Constance.

"No, stay," she said, and for a minute they stood silently, each seeking out the other's thoughts. "I can prove," she went on at last, striving pitifully to control herself, "that our marriage was never binding. And," she added, her breast heaving at the thought, "I can prove that you disgraced me before all these soldiers by refusing to go for water. You are always saying you will love, cherish, and protect me, but, when I went out across the plaza to the fountain, was there anyone there to protect? Certainly it was not you . . . you were hiding like a frightened mouse. And now, after Mister Whittle has risked his life to save me, you come out of your hiding place. . . ."

"Rave on," jeered Pedley with a pitying smile, "rave on if you like to, my child. The point is, I'm still your husband."

A kick at the door broke the ghastly silence, and then Beanie Bogan, his eyes red and dangerous, strode in and looked them over.

"Excuse me, madam," he said, bowing briefly to Constance, and then he turned upon Pedley. "Well," he observed, and his voice cut like a whip, "so here you are again? Yeah, the boys was inquiring about you. You're the brave American that hid in a rag pile while his wife packed water for the wounded. But never mind explaining . . . the job is still open. There's plenty more water to be packed!"

He jerked open the door, and, as Pedley slunk out, Bogan shot a swift glance at Whittle. Then he touched his hat stiffly and stepped out into the court, where the bullets were singing softly of death.

CHAPTER TWENTY-THREE

The swift tide of battle had flared back to the plaza, and the Federals returned triumphantly. They had lost the *cuartel* with its stores of ammunition, but they had driven Espinoso from the heights to the south and cleared half the town of *insurrectos*. They came back in short rushes, driving the *insurrectos* before them, and, as the first of the fugitives poured into the *cuartel*, the Federals swarmed into the church. Then it opened up suddenly, the hail of spattering bullets that went *pinging* across the moonlit patio, and Beanie Bogan, sensing the siege to come, ordered every man to the roof while he brought in water for the wounded. But fighting men were scarce, and, to save them for the pinch, he sent out such as Pedley.

The glare of burning buildings had faded to a glow, and the moon, throwing black shadows beneath walls and archways, cast a ghostly radiance over everything. Whittle stood in the doorway, lis-

tening furtively for he knew not what, and then
he closed the door upon it all. She was looking at
him curiously, but he avoided her eyes—there was
nothing he cared to explain. Yet she sensed it immediately, the cold fear that had clutched his
heart, and glided to his side.

"What is it?" she demanded, "Are they going . . . they won't kill him?"

"No!" he said, but his voice played him false,
and she caught him by the arm. Then he looked
into her eyes and she read the struggle that was
going on in his breast.

"Could you love me," he faltered, "if he should
get killed? They're going to send him for water.
But you couldn't, could you? I can feel it already,
the thought that would come between us. Yet . . . I
hate him so! You don't know how I hate him! But
we must find some other way."

He gazed at her a moment, then dashed out the
doorway and up to the guardroom by the gate. It
was crowded with soldiers and, huddled together
in a corner, stood the men who were to go out for
water. There was a Federal lieutenant who had
broken his parole, a bunch of Mexican looters—
and Pedley, backed up against the wall.

"No, I *won't* go!" he was saying. "You have no
right to force me!"

"*Ahr*, right!" mocked Beanie Bogan, and then he
shifted his eyes as he noticed the entrance of Whittle. "This guy must be a lawyer," he went on bluffly
as Whittle frowned and shook his head. "Well,
what now?" he demanded, striding nervously over
to him. "Why ain't you back there, standing rear

guard?" He listened impatiently as Whittle spoke in his ear, and then he pushed him away. "*Ahr . . . pooey!*" he burst out, pursing his lips in disgust, and Whittle drew him aside again. They were deep in an argument when the crowd opened up, and Constance stepped into the room. She avoided Pedley as he stood, disheveled and glowering, and fixed her eyes on the startled Bogan.

"Sergeant Bogan," she said, "I am going to ask a favor. Please don't send Mister Pedley after water."

Bogan raised his head, shot one baleful glance at Pedley, and brought his heels together. "Very well," he said, and then as an afterthought: "There he is . . . you can take him along."

She went out without answering, but, as Pedley started to follow, he was struck into a heap in the corner.

"Now, you stay here," hissed Bogan, "and, if you move from this room, I'll kill you, so help me God!"

He grabbed Whittle by the arm, rushed him out the door, and gave way to a fit of cursing.

"Out of here!" he yelled, whirling suddenly upon the water squad and menacing them with his uplifted gun. "*Andale*, you bastards! *Vamos par' agua*, or I'll bust ye! Oh, dod rot the whole crazy outfit!"

He glanced dubiously at Pedley, then grabbed up the water buckets and drove the Mexicans out the door.

"Now git!" he ordered, and motioned them toward the plaza, but all the time his eye was on Pedley. Whittle watched him from the distance, then, satisfied at last, he turned and went back to the room.

She was crying softly when he opened the door, but she struck away the tears and rose to meet him with a wistful smile on her lips.

"I'm so glad," she breathed as she met his somber eyes. "We could never be happy with that on our souls . . . love like ours is too sacred to be marred. Perhaps it is too fine to endure for very long, but we must be patient and perhaps, in some way we can't see, God will work it out for the best."

"Yes . . . perhaps," he said as he loosened her hands and led her back to the couch, and then, while she watched him, he paced up and down and fought back the anger in his breast.

She was a woman, she did not know the dark passions that rise up when men fight for love, but as Beanie in his frenzy had cursed the poor water squad, so now Whittle's heart turned against it all.

She spoke of God, but if there was justice in the world, it had not been dealt to Broughton Pedley. He had married this woman against her will, when she was weak from the shock of near drowning and overborne by her mother and her friends, and then, not content with having married her, he was determined to crush her utterly. He had hounded her everywhere, with no thought for her happiness, without an atom of real devotion and love, but merely to appease what he called his honor—his property right in his wife. And he was left safe—nay, protected by everyone—while she, like a tender flower, was being crushed beneath the millstones of convention.

"Constance," he said as a daring thought came over him, "would you run away from it all? I don't know you, really, and you don't know me, but would you trust me and go off somewhere, where no one could find us and we could work out our destiny alone?" He sat down beside her and looked into her eyes that were so wondrous in their ever-changing lights, but now they were suddenly veiled. "I don't mean," he went on hastily, "that we should break any of the conventions, but couldn't we just . . . be friends?"

"No," she answered faintly, "he would follow us everywhere. He is determined to keep up apart . . . to ruin both our lives."

"Then I'll ruin his!" cried Whittle hotly. "That's a game that two men can play. He tried to kill me once, or have me put into prison, and you saw what I did to him then. Well, wait till I meet him again!"

"That was done in self-defense," she reasoned gently, "but you mustn't sink to his level. That's why I despise him . . . he's so material, so brutal, so given over to self-seeking and revenge. But our love must be different . . . if it is to endure through it all . . . be patient and hope for the best."

"But you," he protested, "must you be followed by him everywhere? Must you submit to be called his wife? It is killing you, I know it. It is destroying your soul. You don't care what you do. You say we must be patient, but was that being patient when you went out to the fountain for water? No, you tried to get killed, the same as I did when I thought you were really his wife. . . ."

"I thought you were dead, dear," she broke in very softly, and then her eyes filled up with tears. "Oh, why can't we be happy," she cried, "when we are both here for this one time? Tomorrow I may be gone, or you . . . gone forever . . . but now we are here, together."

"Yes, and he is out there, the dirty swine, groveling down in some corner to save his worthless carcass from a bullet. If I had just said the word, or if I had simply said nothing, he would be out of the way before now, but now I must sit here with both hands tied behind me and remember that you are . . . his."

"No, not his," she flashed back. "Bruce, I want you to love me in other ways . . . won't you put up with it a while, for my sake? Think what I have endured. . . ."

"I do," he burst out, "but why must you endure it any more? You say he loves you for your money . . . then give him the money, and I will get some more. I have five thousand dollars in the bank already . . . isn't that enough for us both? I can work at my trade, and, if you are willing to be poor. . . ."

"Ah, but you don't understand," she cried impatiently. "I have my family to consider, too. They have an honorable name, and, if I should disgrace it. . . ."

"Oh, your family," he said, and then for the first time a flash of anger passed between them. "Well, I have a family, too," he suggested, "a family as good as your own. I am descended from Robert Le Bruce, who became the first King of Scotland. But is that any reason why this pig you call your husband . . . ?"

"That is enough!" she warned, her dark eyes beginning to kindle. "Please do not mention his name again."

"Very well," he said, rising up abruptly, but the black rage of the Bruce was in his eyes. He turned away, and, as he paced the floor, the rattle of .30-30s smote his ears. The boys were fighting, they were up on the roof or shooting from sandbagged windows—and he was quarrelling with a woman. He, the descendant of Robert Bruce, whose heart had been hurled among the Saracens to urge the brave Scottish knights on. "Heart of Bruce," they had cried, "thou wert ever foremost in battle! Lead us on, to victory or to death!"

He picked up his gun and went out.

CHAPTER TWENTY-FOUR

Beanie Bogan was in a fury when Whittle crossed the patio and appeared in the door of the guard-room. He glanced up sharply, then looked again and showed his teeth in a snarl.

"What d'ye want me to do with this damned bag of bull?" he burst out, jerking his head toward Pedley. "They's enough here to do without. . . ."

"I don't care," snapped back Whittle, "what you do with him. You can take him out and shoot him if you want to . . . it makes no difference to me."

Bogan straightened up abruptly and looked his partner over.

"Oh, it don't, eh?" he said, and Whittle's face set hard. "Well," he said at last, "then I've got some work for you . . . we're going to crash the cathedral at dawn."

"All right," responded Whittle, but, as he stood there silently, he felt Pedley's eyes upon him. He glanced up quickly and surprised the cunning scrutiny, the fearful yet leering smile, and a flash of shame mounted to his brow.

"Here!" barked Bogan, striding wrathfully to the corner and bringing Pedley to his feet with a jerk. "Now you beat it . . . git out of here . . . and don't you come back or I'll give some Mex a dollar to shoot you! Out, now!" And he hustled him into the street. "*Pah!*" he spat as he returned to Whittle, and wiped his hand on his leg. "Now forget it," he said with soldierly directness, "and I'll let you in on something big. Everything's going to hell, Whit. Half the boys have deserted me and the Mexicans are down to the bullring. They've got old Bracamonte cornered and they'll never come away until they pay him for killing their wounded. That's the Mexican of it, but I never thought Bill and Helge would go off with all my dynamite. They've slipped back to The Club to blow that safe and make a clean getaway with the loot." He pulled down his mouth at the memory of this treachery but there was an anticipatory glitter in his eyes. "But let 'em go," he whispered hoarsely, "let 'em skip out with the chicken feed . . . the big stuff is with Pepe Montaño. We've got these Federals licked . . . they're waving white rags from the church windows every time their officers turn their backs. The thing now is the grandstand play. We rush the cathedral, see? We storm her at daylight, when we can see to pick off them gunners, and then, when the commander comes out with his sword, we switch in Pepe Montaño. We switch him in, see, and he takes the sword, and then everybody thinks he took the town, but we'll know danged well he was hiding in the *cuartel* and waiting on the fighting Foreign Legion. Are you wise? And when he wins, that puts you and me next . . . we got the contracts to supply him with arms."

Bogan grinned encouragingly and slapped him on the back, and Whittle held out his hand.

"I'm with you," he said. "But how are you going to do it? The boys have gone off with the dynamite."

"Every stick, the dirty rascals," acknowledged Bogan cheerfully, "but the church is dynamite proof, anyhow. Ain't we got that field gun . . . the three-inch Mondragon, right up on the *cuartel* roof? Well, down she comes, steel shield and all, and we load her up with slugs, then we get in behind it and rush her across the plaza, and *blooey* we blow down the door. It's all over then, or I don't know them *pelónes* that have been giving us the high sign with white rags. They'll shoot down their officers and march out and join us, just the way they did here in the *cuartel*."

"But suppose they don't?" suggested Whittle cautiously, and Bogan regarded him with a crafty smile.

"They will," he said. "Never mind how I know it. Well, I'll tell you, then . . . I've got my own men amongst them. Surest thing! I just took them *pelónes* when they come out and surrendered and told 'em what to do. They're the boys that's over there, waving white rags from the windows . . . they went back and threw in with the old bunch. But *a-ah*, listen, boy, when you hear 'em telling how Montaño was in the thick of the fray and how he charged against the Fronteras cathedral that was cram, jam full of Federals! That's the junk, press agent stuff, something to put in the papers . . . and Pepe will give us anything. So off you go now, with a Mexican I'll give you that'll take you straight to Montaño, and, while them crazy Mexicans are butchering Bracamonte, we'll hop in and pull a ten strike."

Whittle went, for the adventure stirred his blood like wine—and he came back with General Montaño. The whole town was in his hands now between the plaza and the river and he had 4,000 men at his back. They were scattered everywhere, but they were armed and under cover, and General Bracamonte was dead. His will it was that had held the Federals together, for he knew that he could hope for no mercy, but now he was dead and the vengeful *insurrectos* were shooting his body full of bullets. Montaño came in through the back entrance of the *cuartel*. He was smiling and the remnant of the legion acknowledged his greetings grimly as they stood by their armored gun.

There were few of them now—less than twenty in all, but they were the pick of the fighting men. Others had fought for loot, or because they had started, but these fought for love of the game. It was the greatest thing in life, the superlative adventure, and they waited impatiently for the dawn. Down the *cuartel* steps they trundled the great gun and turned its nose to the door of the church, and, as the light broke in the east, the Federals looked across and knew that the end was at hand. They had hurried back to the plaza to surround the *cuartel* and eject the presumptuous Americans, but a

night of reckless shooting had lightened their cartridge belts without adding to the dead and
wounded. Bracamonte was gone, and nervous officers with cocked pistols stood behind the half-
mutinous men.

Yet there was business to be attended to before
the charge was made—certain papers for Montaño to sign—and the Army of Liberation came
swarming back to the plaza before Whittle took
his place behind the gun. It was a post of honor,
coveted and clamored for by everyone in the legion, but the best-trained men had to stay behind
to save them from the machine-gun fire. Beanie
Bogan himself took his place on the roof with
spare rifles laid beside him; he posted every man
with strict instructions where to shoot—and then
he raised the yell. The gun crew dashed out, and
crouched behind the steel shield as they trundled
it across the sidewalk, but, as it slumped off into
the street, there came a storm of bullets that beat
against their shelter like hail.

The gun swerved and stuck, the tail bumped
the sidewalk and canted the shield to one side,
and, as they struggled to right it and start it on its
way, two men went down together. Then the
sharpshooters on the roof began to pick off the
gunners and the machine-gun patter suddenly
ceased. A bullet tore the heel from Whittle's boot
as he heaved away at the gun, and then four more
men rushed out from the *cuartel* and put their
shoulders to the wheels. The ground at their feet
seemed alive with bounding bullets, they
smashed and drummed against the steel shield
until it rumbled like thunder, but, although some

went down, the rest rushed on and the cannon went rolling swiftly toward the church. They bumped against the curb, and, looking out through the peephole, Whittle saw the massive doors before them. There were two of them left, and, while his partner clutched the lanyard, Whittle swung the gun about by the tail and sprang back to avoid the shock. The gun went off like a blast, the doors leaped and swayed, and then a great yell rose from across the plaza as the legion began its charge.

"That's enough, boys!" shouted Bogan as he rushed by with the rest.

As white flags flashed out from barred doors and windows, the legion went plunging up the steps. But the battle was won, for as they heaved aside the door a gray-haired colonel stepped out from the darkness with his sword held up in his hand.

"I surrender," he announced in perfect English. "Is there an officer present to whom I can deliver my sword?"

"Where's Montaño?" yelled Bogan, and looked about him wildly, but the general was nowhere in sight. There was an awkward wait, while Bogan rushed back, and then a tall man of military bearing pushed his way through the crowd and saluted the Mexican officer.

"I am Colonel Gambolier," he said, "in command of the Foreign Legion, and I accord you the full honors of war."

"Very well, sir," replied the officer, and handed over his sword just as Montaño stepped out of the *cuartel*.

CHAPTER TWENTY-FIVE

Fronteras had fallen and Montaño had conquered, but the battle was not yet over. The Foreign Legion had fought its way into the city—it had taken The Club, the cathedral, and the *cuartel*—and now, at this moment of its final triumph, its guerdon had fallen to another. The pretender, Gambolier, who had been hiding behind the riverbank giving orders to the *insurrectos* as they went in, had slipped in and received the sword of the commander while his own general was hurrying to accept it. And by that crafty move the well-laid plans of Bogan had been brought to less than nothing. The honor that he had planned to give to Montaño had been filched by the base Gambolier, but, as Beanie burst out into a wild howl of protest, he was silenced by a gesture from his chief. Montaño professed to despise the empty honors of war, but, as he advanced to the cathedral amid the plaudits of his soldiers, he fixed a glittering eye upon Gambolier.

"Colonel Gambolier," he said, "you had no authority to accept the surrender of this town. No, keep the sword . . . it is nothing to me . . . but consider yourself relieved from duty. Sergeant Bogan," he went on, smiling affectionately upon that rough campaigner, "I wish to thank you, as the *de facto* commander, for the work of your gallant legion. Gentlemen," he continued, passing down the thin line and shaking hands with each grimy American, "you have fought like heroes and I shall not forget it. Report to Captain Bogan as your chief."

A swarm of *insurrectos* burst in upon him then and thrust the cheering legion aside. From the doorway of the cathedral the Federals filed out, laughing and stripping off their uniforms. As they passed the little general, they shouted: "¡*Viva* Montaño!" The plaza was filled with their trampled caps, and as they danced with the welcoming *insurrectos*—only the *rurales*, those harriers of the poor, took advantage of the confusion to flee. The Federal band, stripped down to their underwear, came blaring their way through the crowd, and, as they marched up the plaza, a procession fell in behind them and paraded before their chief. The bells of the cathedral *clanged* and *jangled* discordantly, a band of trumpeters sounded *dianas* of victory, and, as the saloons were broken open, the wanton women from the Calle Diablo came running to mingle with the soldiery.

Then the looting began, and, as he sat by the

fountain, Whittle caught his first sight of Bogan.
He was mounted upon a beautiful, blooded horse,
with the brand of Bracamonte on its hip, and, as
he saw Whittle nursing his hurt foot, he reined in
and leaped to the ground with a flourish.

"Well, we win, hey?" He grinned. "What's the
matter with your foot? *Aw,* that's just a bruise . . .
come on, let's get it bandaged, and I'll show you
something big. Here, I'll get you a horse to ride."

He plunged into a group of mounted Mexicans
and grabbed the first horse in sight. The rider
protested violently, but Bogan set him down and
brought the horse back to Whittle.

"Hey, that's my horse!" exclaimed the Mexican,
following indignantly along behind him, and Bogan turned to look at him.

"Oh, it is, eh?" he said. "Well, where did you get
him? Ain't that Bracamonte's brand on his hip?
Well, go on and rustle another one, before I run
you in for looting . . . this horse is too good for a
pelado."

He looked at Whittle's foot, which had been
bruised by the bullet that had taken away the heel
of his shoe, and glanced up to find the Mexican
still glowering. "Here, *hombre,*" he ordered, shoving his pistol forward, "come over here and hold
my horse!"

"*Muy bien,*" returned the looter, "since your
friend is wounded. You are very welcome, I'm
sure." And he held the horse very humbly while
Bogan lifted Whittle into the saddle.

"Now, come on," said Beanie, but, as he started
toward the *cuartel,* he reined in and turned the
other way.

"Where are you going?" protested Whittle, jerking his head and beckoning him toward El Club.

"Never mind," Bogan said. "Don't go in there right now. Come on, the boys are cracking the big safe."

"But why not?" demanded Whittle.

Bogan cursed under his breath as he tried to pass the matter off. "Never mind," he answered. "You listen, to me, for once . . . that's no place for a minister's son."

Whittle checked his horse, and, as Bogan observed it, he whirled and rode back beside him.

"Say, listen . . . ," he began, but Whittle reined away from him and turned and rode for the *cuartel*.

"Is she . . . killed?" he faltered as Beanie spurred past him, but Bogan did not stop to answer. He dismounted at the entrance and ducked into the guardroom, and, as Whittle limped anxiously in after him, he saw him dashing on to the rear. Whittle looked into the guardroom, but there was nothing there such as he feared in his heart to find. Bogan had darted down the passageway where the dead and wounded were carried, and Whittle burst out into a cry of agony. He ran on, unmindful of his bruised and wounded foot, and Beanie met him, coming out a certain door. It was the room for the dead and Bogan pushed him roughly back, but he brushed past him into the room. There they lay, grim forms half covered by blankets, but every one was a man.

"Where is she!" cried Whittle, and, as he faced about, he saw Beanie's eye fixed upon a covered form. He sprang forward, he raised the blanket, and shrank back in a panic—it was Pedley, and he was shot through the head. Just the single bloody spot in the middle of his forehead but it roused something savage in Whittle.

"Who did that?" he raged, but Beanie met his eye with a look of overbearing defiance.

"Now, here," he warned, "I've took about enough already. Don't you look me in the eye and say I did it, because, if you do, you'll be telling a lie. I found him by the window, out there in the guardroom, and he was bored right square through the forehead. Looking out, I guess, when you boys started that gun off, but don't you dare to lay it on me."

Whittle paused and looked at him straight, then he turned and looked at Pedley. It was unfortunate—he was shot in the forehead. "All right, Beanie," he said, and his eyes grew hard as he looked at the dead man again. "Well, that ends it," he said, and, drawing up the blanket, he limped hopelessly out the door.

"Ends what?" demanded Bogan, following along beside him, but Whittle threw up his hands. "Where ye going?" inquired Beanie, and, receiving no answer, he laid a detaining hand on his arm. "Hey, are you going away? Are you going to leave her with . . . that?"

Whittle stopped and looked at him wearily, and at last he shook his head.

"Where is she?" he asked, and Bogan strode past him and knocked on a certain door. He knocked again, then at a sound within he bolted down the corridor and was gone.

Whittle leaned against a pillar and prepared himself to meet her. Did she know—and would she

blame him? They had quarreled—over Pedley—
and then he had snatched his gun and left her
without a word. And now Pedley was lying there,
dead. He glanced at the door, but it had not
opened. She did not wish to see him, of course. He
sat down and pulled on his torturing shoe, and
then started off down the corridor. For days and
nights, he did not know how many, he had been
living in a turmoil of hopes and fears, and now, at
the end, he had lost. She would not even let him try
to explain.

But as he went past her door, it opened softly behind him and Constance Pedley looked out. Her
breast was heaving, her eyes were big with horror,
but her heart went out to him in spite of her.

"Bruce!" she called, and, as he stood there, hes-
itating, she flew down the corridor to meet him.
"Oh, forgive me!" she cried as she caught his
hands in hers. "If it was you, I made you do it. If it
was your hand that murdered him, it was my
word that drove you to it. But, oh, it is awful . . .
awful . . . awful!"

"Yes," he answered, trying to keep his voice
steady, and then, as she seemed to wait upon his
words, he led her gently back and laid her on the
couch. "I know," he began when her sobbing had
ceased, "I know this looks pretty bad, but I tell
you I didn't do it. I don't deny. . . ."

"Oh, no, no," she moaned, "I know you didn't.
It was . . . that terrible Sergeant Bogan. But, oh,
Bruce. . . ."

"No!" he cried. "I accused him myself, but he
swears he never did it. He says he found him
dead, when he came back to the guardroom, after

we made that final charge across the plaza. He gave me his word, Constance ... the word of a soldier ... and I give you mine, as a gentleman."

She looked up, doubting, then at the pain in his eyes she flung herself into his arms.

"Oh, Bruce!" she cried. "Bruce!" And, finding no other words, she besought his forgiveness with a kiss.

In the plaza without, all was rejoicing and tu-mult, but the *cuartel* was quiet as the grave. The dead lay still, for their troubles were over, and, soon they would be forgotten. Burial parties and looters shuffled in and out or hurried past their door, and at last a tall soldier paused. It was Beanie Bogan, his shirt bulging with loot, and, as he listened at the keyhole, his lips parted in a cynical grin. There was a murmur within, of a man and woman, and then it trailed off into si-lence. He shuffled uneasily, then went through his pockets, and fetched out a roll of bills.

"I'll give him half," he muttered. "He was a dan-ged good pardner and ..." He listened again, then looked through the keyhole, and thrust the roll back into his shirt. "Aw, what do they care for money!" he burst out impatiently, and went pound-ing off down the lonely corridor.

ABOUT THE AUTHOR

Dane Coolidge was born in Natick, Massachusetts. He moved early to northern California with his family and was graduated from Stanford University in 1898. In his summers he worked as a field collector and in 1896 was employed by the British Museum in this capacity in northern Mexico. Coolidge's background as a naturalist is a trademark in his Western fiction along with his personal familiarity with the vast, isolated regions of the American West and its deserts—especially Death Valley. Coolidge married Mary Roberts, a feminist and a professor of sociology at Mills College, in 1906. In the summers, these two ventured among the Indian nations and together they co-authored nonfiction books about the Navajos and the Seris. *Hidden Water* (1910), Coolidge's first Western novel, marked the beginning of a career that saw many of his novels serialized in magazines prior to book publication. There is an extraordinary breadth in these novels from *Wunpost* (1920) set in Death Valley to *Maverick Makers* (1931), a Texas Rangers story. Many of his novels are concerned with prospecting and mining from *Shadow Mountain* (1920) and *Lost Wagons* (1923) based on actual historical episodes in the mining history of Death Valley to a fictional treatment of Colonel Bill Greene's discovery of the fabulous Capote copper mine in Mexico, a central theme in *Wolf's Candle* (1935) and *Rawhide Johnny* (1936). *The New York Times Book Review* commented on *Hell's Hip Pocket* (1939) that "no other man in the field today writes better Western tales than Dane Coolidge." Coolidge, who died in 1940, wrote with a definite grace and leisurely pace all but lost to the Western story after the Second World War, although Nelson C. Nye, an admirer of Coolidge, tried in his own fiction to capture this same ambiance. The attention to the land and accurate detail make a Dane Coolidge Western story rewarding to readers of any generation.

HEADING WEST
Western Stories
NOEL M. LOOMIS

Noel M. Loomis creates characters so real it's hard to believe they're fiction, and these nine stories vividly demonstrate his brilliant storytelling talent. Within this volume, you'll meet Big Blue Buckley, who proves it takes a "Tough *Hombre*" to build a railroad in the 1880s and "The St. Louis Salesman" who struggles with the harsh terrain of the Texas prairie. Most poignant of all is the dying Comanche warrior passing on the ways of his people in "Grandfather Out of the Past," a tale that won Loomis the prestigious Spur Award. Each story sweeps you back in time to the Old West as it really was.

ISBN 10: 0-8439-5897-9
ISBN 13: 978-0-8439-5897-3

To order a book or to request a catalog call:
1-800-481-9191
This book is also available at your local bookstore, or you can check out our Web site **www.dorchesterpub.com** where you can look up your favorite authors, read excerpts, or glance at our discussion forum to see what people have to say about your favorite books.

NIGHT HAWK

STEPHEN OVERHOLSER

He came to the ranch with a mile-wide chip on his shoulder and no experience whatsoever. But it was either work on the Circle L or rot in jail, and he figured even the toughest labor was better than a life behind bars. He's got a lot to learn though, and he'd better learn it fast because he's about to face one of the toughest cattle drives in the country. They've got an ornery herd, not much water and danger everywhere they look. The greenhorn the cowboys call Night Hawk may not know much, but he does know this: The smallest mistake could cost him his life.

ISBN 10: 0-8439-5840-5
ISBN 13: 978-0-8439-5840-9

MEDICINE ROAD

WILL HENRY

Mountain man Jim Bridger is counting on Jesse Callahan. He knows that Callahan is the best man to lead the wagon train that's delivering guns and ammunition to Bridger's trading post at Green River. But Brigham Young has sworn to wipe out Bridger's posts, and he's hired Arapahoe warrior Watonga to capture those weapons at any cost. Bridger, Young and Watonga all have big plans for those guns, but it's all going to come down to just how tough Callahan can be. He's going to have to be tougher than leather if he hopes to make it to the post...alive.

ISBN 10: 0-8439-5814-6
ISBN 13: 978-0-8439-5814-0